MACKINAC PASSAGE: THE GENERAL'S TREASURE

Robert A. Lytle

Black-and-white illustrations
Karen Howell

Cover watercolor
Jenifer Thomas

D1227934

MACKINAC PASSAGE: THE GENERAL'S TREASURE

Robert A. Lytle

Black-and-white illustrations
Karen Howell

Cover watercolor
Jenifer Thomas

Thunder Bay Press

Holt, Michigan

Published by Thunder Bay Press
Publisher: Sam Speigel
Designed and typeset by Maureen MacLaughlin-Morris
Black-and-white illustrations by Karen Howell
Printed by Eerdmans Printing Company, Grand Rapids, MI
Cover watercolor by Jenifer Thomas

ISBN: 1-882376-45-5

Printed in the United States of America

97 98 99 2000   1 2 3 4 5 6 7 8 9

ACKNOWLEDGEMENTS

This story, like the others of the *Mackinac Passage* series, could not have been written without the help of a great many people. My several research visits to Mackinac Island have resulted in the renewal of old friendships from my college summer days and the formation of many new acquaintances who, like myself, have a lasting love for all that is Mackinac Island.

They are, in part:

Doug Hobbs, for sharing his historical library and his firsthand experiences with Sugar Loaf Rock. Dr. Eugene Petersen, for his encouraging letters and suggestions for reference materials. Ron and Mary Dufina for lending me their rare copy of *Historic Mackinac*. My wife, Candy, for surprising me last Christmas with my own copy of *Historic Mackinac*. Steve Doud for his unique insight on Mackinac's past and present. Christine Hage, Nancy Bujold, and their staffs at Rochester Hills Public Library for all their support. Linda and Dick Kughn for their generous hospitality at their summer cottage. Susan Groen and Nancy Williams Gram for their letters and calls. Mary Moilanen, Bill and Diane Ebinger, Ken Johnson, and Bob and Gaynor Scruton for their proofreading efforts. Dr. David Armour for his scholarly historical information. Dave Shellenbarger for his computer expertise. My sons, Geoff, Ian, Jamie, and Bo for their patience. And once again, to my sister Karen for her creative sketches that have served to make the *Mackinac Passage* books more enjoyable for all age groups.

DEDICATION

The third *Mackinac Passage* story is dedicated to the people who have come from all over the world to visit Mackinac Island. Be their stay as short as an afternoon call or as long as a lifetime residency, all have discovered Mackinac to be an unforgettable jewel of time and place.

"It's going to be a major slice of heaven."

CHAPTER 1
THE SAIL ACROSS

"Can you believe this?" Kate Hinken said, standing on the deck of the *Griffin*, her long, blond hair waving softly in the morning breeze. "This is great. Clear sky, seventy-five degrees, northwest wind—it couldn't be better."

"Hmm?" Pete Jenkins blinked.

"I said, the weather is perfect," Kate summarized. "It couldn't be better for a sail to Mackinac."

"I still say they're trying to get rid of us," Pete smiled, expression returning to his face. "Why else would they want to get four kids into a fifty-year-old, wooden sailboat and push them into Lake Huron?"

"I don't know," Kate's twin brother, Dan, said seriously. "Maybe they think, if we don't go soon, we'll be scared to sail for the rest of our lives. It's like when you fall off a horse, you're supposed to get right back on or you'll never do it again."

"Whatever the reason," Eddie Terkel, captain of the *Griffin*, said as he pulled the mainsail to the top of the mast, "I'm just glad to go." He looked ahead measuring

1

the wind. He glanced behind him at the dock lined with smiling parents waving from the end of the red, double boathouse. "Kate, hoist the jib. Pete, drop the mooring line. Let's put 'em behind us before they change their minds."

Pete crawled along the deck to the bow and unsnapped the tether. The *Griffin* drifted away from her mooring ball in front of the Cincinnati Row boathouse. The wind slapped the halyards against the wooden mast as the two white sails filled with northern Michigan air. Eddie guided the *Griffin* upwind toward Islington Point. Pete eased back to the cockpit and joined Kate who already was leaning way out over the starboard side.

In the past month sailing had become second-nature to Pete. He couldn't imagine being such a pansy about it before. He loved it now, practically as much as fishing, sometimes even more. Especially when he could be sitting alongside Kate. And why not? Kate Hinken was simply the smartest, prettiest, most awesome girl Pete had ever met. Not to mention, and this is important, she seemed to like him, too. Whatever for, Pete hadn't a clue. Pete Jenkins was a very average kid. His three new friends were fifteen years old, just like Pete, but beyond that, they had nothing in common with him at all. Eddie, Dan, and Kate were high society Cincinnatians. Their parents, grandparents, and probably even their great-grandparents were doctors, lawyers, bankers, and such. Pete, on the other hand, was from Michigan farm stock. His father was a high school agriculture teacher. His grandfather was a lumberjack who farmed the land he had cleared. Pete's great-grandfather was an Irish farm boy who escaped from his country during the potato famine. Pete had grown up distinguishing himself at nothing in particular, certainly nothing that would earn the interest of these resort kids.

In fact, they had met quite by accident, the result of Pete catching a huge muskie in front of their boathouse as they were rigging their sailboat for the weekly regatta. Soon, however, they had taken him into their circle of friends and brought him along as a full partner in their summer activities. They had taught him how to water ski and sail.

Pete stared off into the distance as he thought back. He and his new friends had all come north to their cottages that summer fifteen years old. That much hadn't changed. And it wasn't like anything had happened physically. But he'd sure learned a lot in the past two months. It makes a guy think, you know, being shot at from ten yards away—with a deer rifle, no less. Man, that was close. Fats missed him only because Pete had learned to trust his new friend, Dan Hinken. Dan and his twin sister, Kate, were unlike any kids Pete had ever met. It was like they could read minds and tell the future. Dan had yelled to Pete that day, and Pete jerked his head at just the right moment. The bullet whizzed past Pete's ear and blew out the *Flossy's* windshield. In the next moment, Fats' boat ran aground and blew up in a million pieces. Living through something like that would just naturally make a guy pause and think. Pete thought about stuff he'd never paid any attention to before—clouds, sunsets, waves—everything.

In extremely weak moments, he even found himself thinking how lucky he was to have his big sister, Cara. Now, that was something he'd never thought about before. It would pass, naturally—he hadn't become hopelessly brain-dead—but if Cara hadn't been looking out for him that day, he and his friends would have become holier than a screen door. Fats would have blown a hundred rounds into them as they sat like statues aboard the

Griffin, becalmed at the mouth of Middle Entrance. If there was a hero in all this, it would have to be his sister, Cara.

Pete's short daydreams would occasionally lapse into long trances. When he came out of them, he would look around and see people staring at him. There he'd be, doing some normal thing—fishing, driving his boat, swimming—and suddenly something would remind him of Fats or Mr. Geetings, and just like that, he'd be gone. It wasn't any big deal, normally. Except for the time he was driving the *Tiny Tin* back from Cincinnati Row. He just about rammed the Elliot Hotel pier—in broad daylight, too. Then last week, his sister found him at the end of their dock just staring out across the bay. That, in itself, wouldn't have raised any red flags, except he'd been there for an hour—looking at the water—missed lunch because of it. Well, that got everyone's attention—Pete missing lunch.

Usually, he'd been able to cover up these things. One time it happened while he was on the witness stand at Harold Geetings' trial. Mr. Terkel, Eddie's dad, the lawyer for Mr. Geetings, had asked Pete a question about Fats and, zip, Pete started to daydream about that day on Mackinac. The judge nudged him and Pete woke up. Everyone in the courtroom was looking at him funny, though, like it must have been longer than "zip."

The last thing Pete wanted was to have someone watching over every move he made. There were too many great things to do in the Les Cheneaux Islands—fish, sail, canoe, swim.

So, anyway, Pete was glad when the judge granted a ten-day recess. Dan and Kate's parents quickly suggested that the four teens return to Mackinac Island. They could stay with Dan and Kate's aunt and uncle who lived on the

West Bluff in a huge mansion. Kate, Dan, and Eddie just about jumped out of their shoes, they were so excited. Somehow, everything that had happened in the last month—the murder on Mackinac, the explosion in Bosely Channel, the capture of Fats—none of that had changed his Cincinnati Row friends at all. They still ran around looking for as much mischief as they could possibly get into. Especially Kate. Pete had always been an active kid, but he was kind of on the cautious side when it came to getting into any real danger. Kate, on the other hand, loved intrigue, the more dangerous, the better. In spite of that, or maybe because of it, Pete was dazzled by her every move—her smile, her laugh, her voice, her . . . her . . . everything. Pete would do anything for her, even go back to Mackinac Island, which wouldn't have been his first choice after what had happened there on his last trip. He'd almost rather that she would ask him to jump into a pen of porcupines or wrestle a bear or . . .

"Hello! Pete? Are you with us?" Kate said, shaking his shoulder. "It's time to wake up. We're aboard the *Griffin* on our way to Mackinac. Yoo hoo! Some of us are having fun. Would you care to join us?"

Pete blinked and shook his head. *I've done it again*, he thought. He smiled weakly to his three friends. *What's wrong with me? I can't keep daydreaming like this.*

"Oh, there you are," Kate said smiling. "Now, if it wouldn't be too much trouble, you might haul in on that jib a mite so we can move the *Griffin* up out of trolling speed. This isn't supposed to be an all day sail, you know. We'd like to make it to Mackinac sometime before dinner."

"Oh, yeah. Sorry," Pete said. He tugged sharply on the line he was holding, tightening the forward sail. He glanced at Dan and Eddie who were trying their best to stifle a laugh. Pete looked ahead over the bow. The *Griffin* was already abreast Connors Point a mile from where they'd set sail.

"Besides," Eddie said with a laugh, "I'm in a bit of a rush. There's a cute little waitress at the Chuck Wagon who told me she'd die if I didn't see her soon. So, you may think of this as a mission of mercy, Pete, a sort of higher calling."

"Right, Pete," Dan added, "Dr. Livingstone, here, the great humanitarian, has much work to do. He has many more Island girls to convert unto his beliefs before his mission is complete."

Kate bristled as the boys chortled over their joke.

———

The *Griffin* flew across Muscallonge Bay, out through Middle Entrance, and into the big water of Lake Huron. In five hours, she had skimmed past Goose Island and made her approach to Mackinac Harbor.

The first time Pete had come to Mackinac Island, not quite a month before, he had barely enough time to see anything before Eddie had driven the *Griffin* up on the beach. From that moment on, Pete had done practically nothing but race around Mackinac Island either chasing or being chased by three people he would rather have never seen.

"Pete!" he heard someone say.

Pete glanced along the shoreline with a slightly different outlook than on that first trip. It was still spectacular—the white buildings of the village, the green parks, the horses and buggies, Fort Mackinac, the Grand Hotel, the summer homes on the bluffs—but quickly unforgettable memories of that short stay flooded into his head. His eyes moved to the yacht dock. It was from there that the four had spied on Fats at his apartment. Pete could still feel the dockmaster's furious stare burrowing through him as Pete walked nervously along the pier.

"Pete!"

Pete's view slowly moved to the East Bluff above Mission Point and from there to Robinson's Folly. He felt his stomach churn as he remembered Fats slamming the billy club into the back of Joey Cahill's head. Pete's eyes moved slowly to the left. There, in all of its splendor, was Fort Mackinac where he and Dan had barely escaped from Harold Geetings by stealing the Governor's private carriage and racing away.

"Pete!" Eddie called. "Let off on the jib!"

Pete jumped. The *Griffin* was flying toward the only unoccupied slip in the marina. Pete released the jib sheet, and the wind slipped past the flapping sail. Dan lassoed a piling off to the starboard. Kate snagged a spring line to a port dock cleat. Together, pulling as hard as they could, they brought the *Griffin* to a halt.

"That was close," Eddie whistled. "Where were you, Pete?"

"Sorry. I guess I was thinking of something else."

"No kidding," Eddie said, shaking his head and putting his arm over Pete's shoulder. "Look, Pete, we're here to have fun this time. There's no bad guys to spy on. Dan and Kate's aunt and uncle are putting us up in their cozy little twenty-room cottage and will stop at nothing to see that we don't have a worry in the world for the next week or so. We'll be riding horses, and we won't even have to steal them. We'll be meeting the Governor of Michigan who will be thanking us instead of pressing charges for running off with his carriage. There will be parties—it's going to be a major slice of heaven." He smiled as he pulled Pete toward him and whispered, "So, relax—and don't mess up!"

Pete looked around the marina. A three-piece brass band struck up, "For He's A Jolly Good Fellow," which was being sung by the hundred or so people that lined the yacht dock. George and Nancy Anderson stood in front of the *Griffin* leading the song. The four sailors secured the main sail and stuffed the jib in its bag before stowing it below. Eddie checked the dock lines, and then everyone made their way to the head of the pier. Eight landau carriages were lined up and waiting on the road in front of the Mackinac Island Yacht Club. The Andersons and the honored guests walked through the crowd and boarded the first coach. The driver, wearing a black tuxedo and top hat, cracked the whip and began the parade through town. They proceeded along the route with about a thousand people watching, most of them clutching a camera in one hand and a box of fudge in the other. At the Village Inn the procession turned north and continued up the hill along Market Street. From there they moved along Cadotte Avenue past the Grand Hotel. The parade finally came to a stop in front of the fifth mansion on the West Bluff, the Anderson's "cottage," a misnomer if there ever was one. Pete's place in the Snows was a cottage—two bedrooms, tiny kitchen, small living room, and a quaint little privy about fifty feet out back.

But this place was nothing less than a palace. It was three stories of gleaming white mansion with bay windows, cupolas, and turrets everywhere. Flags, banners, and signs announced the arrival of the Mackinac heroes.

"What's going on?" Pete asked.

"Eddie told you," Dan said. "It's a party in our honor. They think we're heroes."

"What if they find out?" Pete pressed.

"Find out what?" Dan asked in mock astonishment.

"That we're just four lucky, little snoops who were

poking around in something we had no business poking into."

"Oh, that," Dan laughed. "I won't tell them if you won't. Look, let's not spoil their play. It's as much their party as it is ours. Fats' counterfeit money scheme was putting some pretty hefty clamps on a lot of people around here, so they're ready to celebrate, too. Besides, they'd rather look on us as heroes than themselves as morons for being tricked by such a simple scam."

Eddie hopped out of the carriage and held the door. "Come with me, fellow champions of justice, our humble public awaits."

———

The party had already started on the front lawn. The Anderson's domestic staff was dashing around in their black and white uniforms offering *hors d'oeuvres* to over a hundred well-dressed ladies and gentlemen.

After sundown, as the flying bugs and bats began to move in on the party, George Anderson signaled to bring the festivities indoors. Chef Zachary and his staff whisked long, silver trays of beef, fish, and poultry onto a long, linen-covered table. Every imaginable salad and vegetable accompanied the feast. A string quartet entertained by the fireplace. The celebration continued until almost midnight.

"I'm bushed," Pete said to Dan.

"Me, too," Eddie yawned.

"I'll tell Aunt Nancy that we're all going upstairs," Dan said. "We're sleeping in the same rooms we almost stayed in the last time we were here."

In minutes, after saying goodnight to everyone, Pete and his friends climbed the wide, circular staircase to the third floor each going into his own room overlooking the Straits.

Pete pushed open the tall, wide door to his huge bedroom. He stripped down to his skivvies and rolled into the four-poster, goose down-filled bed. He blinked once and was out like the moon on a dark and stormy night.

Twelve-foot breakers charged into Mackinac Island Harbor.

CHAPTER 2
DAY 2 SOU'EASTER

"Pete! Get up!" Dan pounded on Pete's bedroom door. He turned the knob and rushed in. Pete was sound asleep. The long, lace window curtains were brushing his bed. A strong breeze was whistling over the top of the island rustling the balsam trees and rattling the entire, twenty room cottage. "Come on," Dan urged, "we've got to get down to the boat!"

"Huh?" Pete groaned. Pete had never slept in a more comfortable bed in his life. He was practically comatose. He turned his eyes from the door to the window. It was still the dead of night. "What's going on?" he muttered.

"Hurry, Pete!" Dan pressed. "Uncle George got a call from the yacht dock. They're clearing out the marina before it's too late!"

"Too late? For what?"

"A southeaster's blowing up," Dan said, shaking Pete's shoulder. "We have to move the *Griffin*. Come on."

"Move the *Griffin*? Where?" Pete asked, burrowing deeper under the covers.

"To the other side of the Island," Dan insisted. "If we don't go right now, we won't have a boat to go home in."

Pete rolled out of bed and fell into his clothes. He stumbled along in his untied moccasins following Dan down the stairs. Eddie and Kate were already in the living room dressed and ready to go as Aunt Nancy was carrying out a tray of toasted English muffins from the kitchen. Eddie glued two halves together with about an inch of strawberry jam. Seeing Dan and Pete coming down the stairs, he started for the back door.

"Hurry up, guys," he said. "We can eat on the way."

The four house guests hurried through the kitchen, threw open the back door, and ran across the dew-filled lawn to the stable. Eddie slid open the barn door and each grabbed a bike. They hopped on and raced along the back road in the pre-dawn chill past the Grand Hotel golf course. A crisp, clear, crescent moon flooded light on the ghostly clouds of fog that shimmered in patches from the wet fairways. They pedaled behind the Governor's Mansion down Fort Street past Doud's Grocery. The street washers were just turning off the fire hydrants and putting away their hoses in front of the Chippewa Hotel as the four bikers shot toward the yacht dock. They dropped their bikes at the head of the marina and ran toward the pier.

A sixty mile-an-hour gale hit them smack in the face as they struggled along the dock to the *Griffin*. Twelve-foot breakers charged up Lake Huron and barrelled into Mackinac Harbor. Gigantic whitecaps smashed against the breakwalls sending great flumes of white water forty feet into the air. The wide, wooden pier shook riotously with each wave. Pete slipped and fell twice as he ran along the bouncing dock. Yachts, held in their slips with long, thick lines, were being tossed around like rubber toys in a bathtub.

"She's still building," Steve, the dockmaster, hollered over the shrieking gale. "She's been swinging around from due east all night. Pretty soon, she'll be right out of the southeast. Nothing will stop her from blowing everything up on shore. You'd better get your boat out of here now. Practically everyone's left for British Landing."

"Thanks," Eddie hollered. "Can you give us a hand getting off?"

"Not right now," Steve said, shaking his head. "Some single-handed boats are still trying to get out. I've got to help them first. Besides, it looks like you brought a crew." Steve turned. "I've got to run. Good luck!"

Just then, in the well next to them, a stern line snapped from the *Heidi Ho*, a forty-two foot Matthews. The four *Griffin* sailors watched as Steve raced to the luxury cruiser, its engine roaring in neutral. The stern whipped back and forth bashing into the finger pier on one side and the pilings on the other. A twelve-foot wave thrust the *Heidi Ho*'s bow high out of the water and dropped it on the dock. The boat hung for a moment, and then, as the wave passed, it slid from the pier into the trough. A gaping hole opened up two feet above the water line. The next wave poured gallons of water into its cabin.

A thin, elderly man at the helm hit the throttle trying to straighten it in its slip. A tall, white-haired woman scurried frantically along the deck shouting instructions to the man at the helm while untying lines from the *Heidi Ho*'s cleats. Steve rushed to the finger pier and cast the last bow line onto the foredeck. The boat drifted backwards toward shore as the old man gunned the engines. Slowly, the *Heidi Ho* began to make its way toward the west end of the pier.

"Let's get out of here," Eddie yelled.

The four picked their way along the dock jumping over snapping ropes and power cables. As they approached the *Griffin*, they could see that, so far, she was in no immediate danger. Eddie had made certain, even with all the fanfare of their arrival the day before, that the *Griffin*'s dock lines were set correctly. He'd been in this harbor before and knew what a southeaster could do.

In the slip next to the *Griffin*, a 28-foot Egg Harbor lurched from side to side straining at the dock cleats with every wave. Alone at the front of the boat sat a slightly-built, thin-faced woman who braced her feet on the deck and held the bow lines like a bronco-busting, rodeo rider. She wore a yellow rain slicker and strained with each surge of the boat. She was trying desperately to keep the ropes from snapping, but it appeared to Pete that it wouldn't be long before she would snap, herself.

"You're not staying, are you?" Eddie called out to the lady as he stood beside the *Griffin*.

"Got to," she hollered back. "Clogged fuel line."

Eddie shook his head and jumped aboard his sailboat.

Pete stood on the dock and pulled the *Griffin*'s stern line bringing her close enough to let Kate and Dan join Eddie.

"Be ready to untie the bow lines, Pete," Eddie yelled. "The three of us will get the sails set. When we're ready, toss us the lines and hop in. We'll fend off the pilings and back her out. Once we're free of the dock, we'll hoist the sails and tack upwind. Got it?"

Pete nodded and glanced at the woman struggling alone on the boat next to him. She could never make it through the storm—not the way she was going. In minutes, Dan, Kate, and Eddie had the *Griffin* rigged, the sails snapping loudly in the wind.

"We're ready, Pete," Eddie hollered. "Take that spring line once around the piling and hand it to Kate. Kate, hold on 'til I tell you. Okay? Now, Pete, do the same with the bow line and hand it to Dan. Got it, Dan?" Eddie turned and looked nervously at the huge waves rolling into the harbor. "I think we're ready," he yelled. "When I say 'go,' I'll drop the two stern lines. You two bring in the bow and spring lines, and Pete, you jump aboard. Okay?"

Pete glanced back to the woman next to him. "I'll help you get off, Eddie," he yelled, "but I think you can do the rest without me. This lady's not going to make it without some help."

Eddie looked at the woman in the power boat who was grimacing with each wave. He nodded. "You're right, Pete. Besides, we might be better off with just the three of us, anyway. Wish us luck," he screamed back. "Ready, everyone?" Dan and Kate nodded. "Go," Eddie called.

Everyone cast their lines and pushed against the fenders and pilings to move the *Griffin* out of her slip. Eddie pushed the tiller, and the bow turned into the violent wind. The *Griffin* plunged down into the trough of an eight-foot wave. She flew high out of the water and crashed hard into the next swell. It hurled Eddie against the deck. He smashed his head on the boom but somehow managed to control the tiller. Kate flew off her feet and landed in the cabin. She scrambled out and fought her way forward to hoist the jib. The small sailboat dropped into another trough, and with the next wave Dan flew on his face in the cockpit.

Pete watched helplessly as his three friends banged around like ping-pong balls in a bouncing box. Slowly, Eddie brought the *Griffin* toward the white rocks of the west breakwall. Pete stood watching on the dock tensing with each wave. All it would take would be one slip, one blink, one wrong decision and his three friends would be washed overboard and drowned.

15

Fifteen minutes later, a time which seemed like hours, the *Griffin* nosed up to the point of the rocky breakwall.

"Ready about!" Eddie yelled. Kate and Dan jumped from the port to the starboard. "Hard alee!" Eddie shouted. He pushed the tiller, and the boom whistled over the three sailors' heads. The main sail billowed shooting the *Griffin* downwind like a rocket. Pete lost sight of the boat and could see only the top of the mast as it flew north in the lee of the breakwall. His friends were safe. At least, for now.

Once they were out of sight, Pete glanced at the slip beside him. The woman continued to strain as each wave crashed into her powerless power boat.

She looked at Pete. "That was close," she called. "I wouldn't have given them one chance in a million the way they started out."

Pete just nodded. "Need some help?" he yelled back.

"Sure," she said. "With your friends' sailboat gone, you could lengthen my lines. Here, undo this one and tie it over there," she pointed to a dock cleat that the *Griffin* had left open. "Now, take this one over there." Soon, Pete had retied all eight lines and put four new ones out as the savvy woman remained at her post and gave directions.

Soon her boat was rising and falling in its well with much more stability than it had only minutes before. Still, she struggled with the bow lines laboring with each wave. The force of the wind was increasing and coming now straight from the southeast. Her twenty-eight foot cruiser was, even more than before, at the mercy of the gale.

Pete looked up to survey the chaos in the rest of the harbor. Off to his right he watched a fourteen-foot Thompson outboard being tossed in the wind. Three of its lines had snapped. Only one long stern rope held it a mere twenty feet from the sharp boulders that lined the shore. The transom took on water with each passing wave.

A man stood in the stern, ankle-deep in water. He pulled desperately at the starting cord of his twenty-five horse-power, Johnson motor. And then it happened. The anchor line snapped. Immediately, the stern spun sideways and the next wave swamped the small craft.

The shore was lined with people who watched in horror as the man leaped from the boat. He surfaced a few feet from shore, his head bobbing out of the water and his mouth open screaming for help. The next surge picked the man up like a stick figure and slammed him against a table-sized block of white limestone. In desperation, he reached out to grab the rock before the undertow could suck him back into the depths. Two young people, a boy and a girl, seized his arm and shirt. The next wave crashed over the jagged boulders slapping all three of them ten feet ashore onto the grass lawn. The man rolled to his knees straightening up just in time to see his fishing boat dashed into kindling wood fifteen feet away.

Pete stared, still standing on the dock. His mind drifted back a few weeks to Robinson's Folly and Fats bashing Joey Cahill with a club.

"If you're willing," the woman yelled over to Pete, "I could use a break."

"Oh, yeah, sure," Pete said, blinking. He hurried along the finger pier and pulled the woman's cruiser close enough to the dock to jump aboard. He timed his leap with the next swell and landed on the deck. He worked his way, hand over hand, along the stanchions toward the bow.

"If you could keep these lines from snapping," she said, making room for Pete to sit next to her, "I'd like to go below and see what I could do in the cabin. I can't thank you enough for helping. With everything that's going on up at the Annex, I don't think I could stand to lose my boat."

17

"Sure," Pete shouted. "How long's this likely to go on?"

"The last weather report said it could last all day with rain coming late this afternoon."

"Oh, no," Pete moaned.

"No," she called back. "Rain would be good. It flattens down the waves." She handed the two bow lines to Pete and stood up. Slowly, she inched her way to the cabin and went below.

Pete soon got into a rhythm of pulling on the ropes just as the next wave hit. He looked across the marina. What a mess. Of the thirty boats that were docked the night before only six remained. Lines were stretched out everywhere. Pilings had snapped and cleats were torn out leaving ropes dangling in the water.

Pete looked to his right and noticed a life ring next to him attached to the starboard stanchion. Black letters spelled the boat's name, "Sea Gal." Pete put two and two together. *So this lady is the owner*, Pete thought. *From what she said, she must have a cottage up at the Annex, too. Some of the guests at last night's party had said they were from the Annex. What could be going on at a ritzy, Mackinac Island resort area that would be worse than losing your boat? Well, it's not my problem.*

He began to think about the rest of his week's stay at the Anderson's place. He figured he could adjust to living in a house that came with a maid, a butler, a chef, and who knows how many other people he hadn't even seen. They'd be only too anxious, he was sure, to do anything his little heart desired. Not that he'd had the opportunity to try, as yet, but given the time and some imagination, he was sure he could make darn good use of all those servants. He was totally into the concept of being waited on hand and foot when the rains started.

"Here's a slicker," the lady called out from beside him. "You, know, I don't even know your name. I'm Edna Fisher."

Pete blinked. "I'm Pete. Pete Jenkins," he said, recovering quickly from his short lapse of concentration. "Thanks. I hadn't even noticed the rain. How long's it been coming down like this?"

"A while now," she replied. "You know, you're a regular workhorse, Pete. I don't know what I'd have done without you. But if this rain keeps up, we may have seen the worst of the storm. The noon forecast an hour ago called for a wind shift by three o'clock. Let's hope so. Here, I brought you a sandwich. We're lucky the tuna fish and bread weren't breakable or we'd have starved. If you're okay I'll go around the boat again and adjust the lines."

"Yeah, I'm fine," Pete said, putting on the rain coat. "Thanks for the sandwich."

The sun shone brilliantly over the rain-soaked village.

CHAPTER 3
RETURN

Shortly after four o'clock in the afternoon, twelve hours after Pete and his friends had come to the dock, the rain stopped and the wind shifted further to the south. The waves began to subside but still pounded the *Sea Gal* for another hour. By five o'clock the sun emerged brilliantly in the northwest over the peaceful Mackinac Island village.

By six o'clock there wasn't a hint of a storm—except, of course, for the devastation in the harbor. Three boats remained in the marina: the forty-eight foot Pacemaker, *Delicado*, looking as if it had passed unsuccessfully through a mine field, a black-hulled Chris-Craft, the *Weak Moment*, which didn't look much better, and the *Sea Gal* which rose and fell gracefully in her slip without a scratch anywhere. Pete Jenkins, however, sat at his station looking as though he had been dragged by his hair through an entire war.

Boats began to return from the anchorage on the other side of the Island, and soon the slips that were usable were almost all filled. Pete looked up and watched the *Griffin* approach. Kate waved and called out to him.

"Hey, Pete, give us a hand," she yelled.

Pete jumped up and cleated the two *Sea Gal* ropes he'd been holding for the past twelve hours. He crawled along the deck and leaped from the small cruiser onto the finger pier.

"How'd it go, Pete," Kate yelled, tossing him a line.

"Pretty good, I guess." He wrapped the hemp rope around the base of the dock cleat and then formed a "figure eight with a twist" over the top. `That'll hold the *Queen Mary*,' Eddie had told him on his first sailing lesson.

"How'd it go with you?" he asked.

"British Landing was protected from the wind, all right," Eddie said, "but the swells came around both sides of the island and kept us bouncing all day like we were trapped in a tornado."

"This is incredible," Dan said, glancing around the harbor. "I'm sure glad we got out when we did."

"Well," Pete replied, "no one around here seemed to be lacking for things to do, I'll say that."

Edna Fisher stepped from her cabin and stood on the bow surveying her boat.

"Oh, Pete," she called out. "I see your friends made it back." She turned to those aboard the *Griffin*. "I don't know how I can repay you for letting me borrow Pete for the day." She turned to Pete. "Pete, I'd like to invite you and your friends to my place in the Annex for dinner one night soon."

Pete glanced at Dan who's eyes were alight. "Okay," Pete replied to the woman. "Sure, that'd be great."

"How about tomorrow night, then. Seven o'clock," she smiled. "It's the white one in the Annex overlooking the west bluff. Do you know how to get there?"

Pete looked at Dan. Dan nodded. "I know right where it is," Dan answered.

"That's splendid," Edna Fisher said. "I look forward to seeing you then."

Edna turned and went back into her cabin.

"Do you know who that is?" Dan whispered to Pete.

"Yeah," Pete said with a shrug. "Her name is Edna Fisher."

"There's a lot more to it than that," Dan said slowly. "Let's get squared away. I've got to tell Aunt and Uncle about this. Come on."

They walked their bikes up to the Grand Hotel.

CHAPTER 4

The four weary sailors made their way up Cadotte Avenue walking their bikes the last hundred yards of the steep incline until they'd reached the Grand Hotel Snack Bar. They hopped back on their bikes and pedalled behind the big hotel until they reached the West Bluff service road. At the fifth carriage barn, they turned in and parked the bicycles inside. They walked across the path and into the back door of George and Nancy Anderson's cottage and into the living room. There, Dan and Kate's aunt and uncle were sitting looking out over the West Bluff at the late afternoon sky.

"Oh, good," Nancy Anderson said, folding a book in her lap. "Dinner will be ready in half an hour."

"Great," Dan responded. "I've been running on empty since noon."

"How did everything go with the *Griffin?*" George Anderson asked.

"We survived," Kate said. "We had to anchor off British Landing with about thirty other boats. Pete had an interesting day. You'll never guess who he spent it with—Edna Fisher."

"Really?" Aunt Nancy looked surprised. "Are you sure?"

"It was Edna Fisher, all right," Dan said.

"What's so special about Edna Fisher?" Eddie asked.

"She's the daughter of Lemuel T. Fisher," George Anderson said. "He was a Civil War general, lumber baron, poet, and philosopher—a grand, old gentleman. He built one of the first cottages in the Annex in the 1880's. He died around 1915. Edna has lived here all her life, but practically no one ever sees her. How she does that on an island this small is a mystery to me."

"Well, get this," Dan continued, "she's invited us for dinner tomorrow at her place in the Annex."

"I declare," Nancy Anderson said. "You four certainly have a knack for getting into the most uncommon situations."

"That is extraordinary," George Anderson followed. "What did you do to deserve this?"

"Pete helped her at the yacht dock all day," Kate said.

"You were with her all day?" Nancy asked. "What was she like? What did she say?"

Pete was surprised by all the interest in his new friend. "Uh, not much," Pete replied to the last of the flurry of questions. "We were pretty busy just keeping her boat in one piece."

"Her boat?" George questioned. "What boat is that?"

"It's called the, uh, *Sea Gal*," Pete answered.

"That old Egg Harbor is hers?" George asked. "I've seen it at the dock but never with anyone aboard. She sure can keep a secret like no one I've ever met. Or I should say, never met."

"You've never met her?" Kate asked.

"Not really," Uncle George answered. "In all my years on the Island I've only seen her twice—at her father's funeral over thirty years ago and at her sister's funeral last month. They're both buried in Bonnie Brae Cemetery north of the Fort."

"Edna Fisher had a sister?" Dan asked. "I never heard about her."

"Yes," George Anderson replied. "Her name was Alexa. She was three years younger than Edna. She married, had a son, and lived in a remote part of Bois Blanc Island. It wasn't a very happy marriage, I gather. It seems her husband, Ed Sawyer, didn't like all the social activity here on Mackinac. He was a moody cuss, too, obsessed with searching for some kind of treasure that he thought was buried there. You know, I believe there's a book at the library that tells about the Fisher family. The General wrote it himself. Tomorrow, you might go down there and ask to see it. At least, it would give you something to talk about at dinner tomorrow night with Miss Fisher."

The door to the kitchen opened and Zachary, the chef, entered the living room. "Dinner will be served in twenty minutes' time," he said with a bow.

"We'd better freshen up," Dan said, flashing a smile at Pete.

The others followed up the stairs to their rooms.

"Fudgies—one-day tourists. The place is lousy with 'em by noon."

CHAPTER 5
DAY 3 MORNING

Pete looked up from his prone position perhaps three to four inches into the world's largest and most comfortable bed. His eyes followed the lines of the high ceiling to the tall windows that overlooked the Straits of Mackinac. The lace curtains swirled in little eddies as the cool air circulated throughout his room. A horse clomped by on the dirt path below.

Can this be for real? Pete thought.

A faint twinge of hunger brought him back to earth. *I wonder if the others are awake. I wouldn't want to miss going with them into town.* He pulled back the covers and hopped out of bed. He dressed and went into the hallway. Dan, Kate, and Eddie's doors were all open. He made his way down the stairs and found them sitting at the long, dining room table. Pete pulled out the chair with the needlepoint picture of Fort Mackinac and sat down next to Kate.

"Good morning, Sleepy-head," Kate said as she pressed a silver button on the wall. Pete could hear a bell ring in the back part of the house. "We've been waiting for you."

"We thought we'd give you one morning to sleep in," Dan said. "But don't count on it happening again. This is the best part of the day for getting around and doing things. After noon there are so many fudgies that you can hardly move."

"Fudgies?" Pete asked.

"Tourists," Eddie replied. "One-day visitors. They come from all over the world, board a boat in St. Ignace or Mackinaw City in the morning, and descend on the Island like lemmings. The place is lousy with them by lunchtime. They take pictures, eat fudge, and buy souvenirs like there's no tomorrow. Then they ride around on rented bikes and horse carts and take one of the last boats off the Island in the afternoon."

"Kind of like us, last time we were here," Pete smiled.

"We didn't bring cameras," Dan corrected.

"And I sure didn't get any fudge," Eddie added.

"A lot of people," Dan said, "come here because there aren't any cars. It's kind of a novelty. They know they can walk anywhere and not get flattened by a truck. They spend an afternoon going through Fort Mackinac, walk over to Arch Rock and up to the Grand. When they leave they think they know all there is to know about this place when really, they haven't even scratched the surface."

"So we like to get out early," Kate added. "The library opens at nine. Miss Martin will be able to show us the book Uncle George told us about last night."

A lady in a black uniform and white apron appeared outside the dining room with a tray loaded with juices, fruits, and pastries. She set it on the table and handed each of them a napkin and silverware.

"Will there be anything else?" she asked.

"I don't think so, Mrs. Odin," Dan replied. "We'll ring when we're finished. Thank you."

27

"So," Pete said, picking out a hot, cinnamon Danish, "if it's not the fudge and the no-cars, what *does* make Mackinac Island so special?"

"One word, Pete, `History,'" Eddie said, reaching for a steaming Bismarck. "Mackinac is probably the most important island in all of North America. First, for the Indians, it's their Eden, the birthplace of their people. When the European explorers, missionaries, and fur traders came, Mackinac became the center for everything they did. The French controlled it for a long time, then the British, and then the United States got it. It's been the most famous resort spot in North America ever since."

"There, Pete," Kate said, setting down her juice glass, "let's get started."

"I'm all set," Pete said, stuffing the last of his cinnamon Danish into his mouth. "Let's go before the fudgies get here."

CHAPTER 6
"THIS FAIRE ISLE"

In minutes, the four had swept down into town on their bikes and pulled up to the library on Market Street. It was nine o'clock and the only people walking along the street were summer workers wearing old-fashioned costumes to their jobs. It was kind of eerie, Pete thought, as if he had just been whisked back two hundred years in time.

Miss Martin was just unlocking the door to the library and awakened Pete from his daydream.

"Dan, Kate," she said, swinging the screen open. "Come in. What brings you to the library on such a perfect day? I don't usually see you unless it's raining."

"We need your help," Kate replied. "We're going to a dinner party tonight up at the Annex. Uncle George said that you might have a book that could tell us about the family we're visiting."

"Well, if it's written and it's about the Island, I've got it," Hazel Martin beamed. "Where's the party?"

"Edna Fisher's," Dan answered.

"Oh," the young librarian's smile fell from her face. "I'm afraid I can't help much. Last week, two of our most prized books were stolen. One was the memoirs of General Fisher, Edna's father. And the other was *This Faire Isle*, a book of the General's poems. Whoever stole it got one of only two known copies." Her face brightened slightly. "Luckily, I kept the other in our safe."

"Who would have done such a thing?" Kate asked. "Were they worth a lot of money?"

"No," Miss Martin said. "As rare as they were, they were only valuable for historical sake. General Fisher was a brilliant military leader, but after the war he pretty much stayed here on Mackinac until he died in 1915. He spent all his time with his two daughters and wrote his thoughts about the Civil War. The government gave him almost half of Bois Blanc Island five miles south of here as payment for his service to his country. He sold that and built one of the first homes in Hubbard's Annex. He brought his young wife and two daughters, Edna and Alexa, and never left Mackinac Island again."

"He must have made a fortune," Dan said, "in order to live without working the rest of his life."

"He did," Miss Martin agreed. "The timber rights alone were worth more than any one person made from the California Gold Rush. And from what I understand of his lifestyle, he certainly didn't spend it here. He lived very simply devoting all of his time to his family and to reading and writing."

"Let's get back to the missing library books," Dan persisted. "Who do you think stole them?"

"I've got a hunch," Hazel Martin said. Her eyes tightened and her jaw set. "There's only one person who could have wanted those books."

"It wouldn't be Edna Fisher," Eddie guessed.

"No, not Edna," the librarian said, shaking her head. "I think it's her nephew, Ronald Sawyer. He's come to stay with Edna since his mother died last month. He's been here three weeks now. One day he came in here wanting to know about his grandfather. Legend has it that General Fisher left a treasure which has never been found. Ronald made me a little nervous, the way he was demanding so much, but I showed him the books. Then he grabbed for them as though he intended to take them. I told him that reference materials could not leave the library, and he became very angry. He said he had a right to them, that they were his. I told him that he could read them all he wanted, but they were willed by General Fisher to the library. He stalked off, but later when I went to close the library, the books were gone. I think he sneaked back and stole them. There is something else about him, too. I wasn't sure at first, just a feeling, but I don't believe he's completely all there mentally."

"Could we see the book you keep in the safe?" Kate asked.

"Yes, of course," Miss Martin said with a weak smile. "You won't mind if I stay with you while you look at it. Having lost those two books, I feel as though I've let down all the other Mackinac Island librarians who have cared for them over the years. I'd do anything to get them back."

She walked over to the shelves marked "Mackinac Island" and pointed out the two spaces where the stolen books had been kept.

"Isn't there anything you can do to make Ronald Sawyer return them?" Kate asked.

Miss Martin shook her head. "Not that I know of," she answered.

"I bet if I got my hands around his miserable neck, he'd tell us where they are," Eddie growled.

"I have no proof," Hazel Martin said. "I saw him on the street the next day and asked him if he had taken them.

He just said, `Maybe I did. Maybe I didn't. What are you going to do about it?' And then he laughed and walked away to the pool hall above Horn's Bar. Well, he's right. I can't do anything about it. At least not now." Miss Martin moved to the safe and spun the dial. "But you can be sure this book isn't going anywhere." She turned the brass handle and the safe opened. She reached inside and withdrew a beautiful, leather bound book. The words, "This Faire Isle," gleamed in gold letters. Under it was the inscription, "The Poems of General Lemuel Fisher."

They concentrated on a poem about Dwightwood Spring.

CHAPTER 7
GENERAL FISHER'S GIFT

The four sat together at the library table with Miss Martin placing the book between Dan and Kate.

"I've read this, beginning to end, three times," the librarian smiled. "I think you'll learn most about what you're looking for, though, in the introduction. General Fisher wrote it sitting right here at this desk. The poems, as far as the meter and rhyming patterns are concerned, are very well written. Their content, however, is painfully predictable. Each deals with different places on the Island, be they of historical or natural interest. They always end with a moral reference or a Biblical lesson of some kind. General Fisher was a deeply religious man and a hopeless romantic. He found something beautiful in every rock and view."

Kate turned to the front and the four bent over the book. It read:

"Introduction
I choose this old and oaken desk to preface
now these rhymes describing God incarnate on

33

this Island. As a general in the Civil War I sent my young and robust soldiers into battle. Often they returned on bloody litters, broken, sick, or lifeless in retreat. A vital part of me succumbed with every young man's passing.

After Appomattox more of me was dead than was alive. By fate, my post-war charge did bring me here upon this fairest of all isles. And though, so far away from native home, I found that God bestowed my life anew.

Within this Island's bosom here I felt the fresh and earnest strength to live again; I found a cause worth all the pain and death my men had suffered. I vowed to live my life in celebration of God's love.

I herein give my thanks to Him for all these vibrant days. I leave my heirs sufficient wealth, secure their wants are safely met, for elsewhere have I placed reserves that will provide their life-long needs.

But to life's melancholy travelers who, by God's own will, have wandered hither to these shores, I leave these rhymes. It is the culmination of my life, my gift to all whose souls, like mine, were once forlorn, then lifted high upon His mighty hands.

Herein, I pen my contemplations of this place, a magic Island on God's magic Earth—for those whose hearts are burdened, carry as a thimbleweight, the golden treasures of this land.

General Lemuel Fisher,
United States Army, Retired"

"Oh, he could turn a word," Miss Martin swooned.

The four friends sat at the table gathered close to the small, leather book. Pete glanced out the window, his attention wandered toward a bird chirping atop a nearby hemlock branch.

Miss Martin leaned over Pete's shoulder and turned the page. Pete snapped his head almost cracking the librarian in the jaw. He glanced around blinking like he'd been in a deep sleep. The others were concentrating on a two stanza poem about Dwightwood Spring. Pete wiped the sweat from his forehead and tried to concentrate on their conversation.

"Well," Dan said, getting up from his chair. "I guess that gives us about all we need for our party with Edna Fisher tonight. Thanks for letting us see the book, Miss Martin."

"Sorry about the two that were stolen," Kate added. "If we find out anything about them at the party, we'll let you know."

"Thanks, kids," Hazel Martin said. "But I don't think there's anything you can do." She set the book in the safe and spun the dial.

As Eddie pushed open the library door a finch flew off into the woods. Pete followed the others past the hemlock tree and jumped on his bike. They all waved to Miss Martin and headed back up to the West Bluff cottage of George and Nancy Anderson.

"There are still lots of bones way back in there."

CHAPTER 8
HORSEBACK

"What does everyone want to do now?" Dan asked after closing the barn door.

"You mean after lunch?" Pete said.

"It's too soon for that," Kate answered. "We've still got an hour or so before it's ready. Let's give Uncle George's horses some exercise."

"You take the horses for walks?" Pete asked.

"You can take yours for a walk, Pete," Kate smiled. "I'm taking mine for a run. Let's find Uncle George."

It suddenly occurred to Pete, *She's not expecting me to walk beside a horse. Or even run with it. Kate actually expects me to ride a horse. I think she's just figured out another way to kill me.*

———

"Uncle George, may we take the horses out for an hour?" Kate asked as the four came into the Anderson's living room.

"Sure, any time, you know that," George Anderson said. "Come with me. I'll go with you to the barn. It's a fine morning for a ride."

"Thanks, Uncle George," Dan smiled. "Come on, guys."

Pete trailed behind as George Anderson led the way out back. Uncle George opened a different door than where the bikes were kept, and the five entered the horse barn. They passed four empty stalls and went out into a fenced-in field. In the distance, near an old maple tree, four chestnut brown, Morgan horses stood glistening in the sun. A tall, darkly tanned man wearing rubber waders was pitching hay from a mow into a large feeding trough. He looked up as Uncle George slid the door to a stop. He planted his pitchfork into the hay and began walking toward the new arrivals.

"William, would you help the kids get saddled?" Mr. Anderson said. "It looks as though you've got them all fed, watered, and raring to go."

"You bet, Mr. Anderson," the hostler said with a smile. This would take care of one of his daily duties. He normally exercised the horses himself by riding one and having the others follow, tethered, as they walked the back riding paths of the island.

In fifteen minutes the four horses were saddled. In a blink of an eye, Kate, who was standing next to Pete, was suddenly sitting tall on her mount. *How in the world did she do that?* Pete wondered. She smiled at Pete as her horse whinnied and chomped at the bit. Pete stood beside his horse and looked up at the stirrup. The saddle seemed to be half a story high, and his horse now looked to be more the size of an elephant than the sleek, graceful animal he'd seen from across the field. He watched as Dan grabbed the horn of his horse's saddle. He gave a little jump to the stirrup, caught it with his left foot, and swung his right leg over the top.

That looks easy enough, Pete thought, *I can do that.*

Next, it was Eddie's turn. Eddie stretched high to get his left foot into place. He bounced once, twice, three times on his right foot. He groaned as he strained to hoist himself up to the saddle and nearly slid off the other side before settling in. Pete quickly lost what little confidence he had gained from watching Dan.

"Need a hand up?" William asked.

"Huh?" Pete said, turning to the man.

"Would you like me to give you a boost?" William rephrased his offer. "Your horse's name is Chester. Here, let me get you started."

"Oh, yeah, thanks. I've never done this before," Pete mumbled.

"Really," William said with a smile.

William's shoulders under his tan work shirt were huge. His neck and back were wide, and when he cupped his hands to give Pete a lift, it was as if he could have supported all four of the kids at once.

"Put your foot here, Pete," William said. "No, your other foot. You wouldn't want to be facing south if Chester was heading north, now, would you?" he smiled and his leathery face practically cracked along its deep, furrowed lines.

"No, I guess not," Pete responded to the good-natured taunt. He took the hand up and swung his leg over Chester's back. His foot splayed out to the side before he got it into the stirrup. The horse glanced backwards at Pete as if sizing him up to see how far he could throw him. Pete, convinced he was about to be launched into Lake Huron, grabbed the horn of the saddle and held on for dear life.

"Take the reins, Pete," Kate called out.

Pete grabbed the leather straps and his horse began to walk forward.

"Stop!" Pete yelled, his eyes flashing.

"Relax, Pete," Dan said, "you're doing fine. Chester's the most gentle riding horse on the Island. He's not going to throw you, honest."

"Thank you, William," Kate waved as she led the party through the gate. "We'll be back in an hour."

"I didn't think horses were this tall," Pete said to Dan. "I feel like I'm sitting on a giraffe or something."

"You'll get used to it," Dan assured him. "It's like when you learned how to water ski. Once you got the hang of it, it was a breeze, right? Just watch, before long, you'll be wanting to race us."

"Right," Pete said, trying to forget that first skiing lesson. Just the mention of it, though, sent a chill up and down his spine. If Dan was trying to encourage him, he couldn't have picked a worse fr'instance. Pete gripped one hand on the reins and clenched the other to the saddle horn. "Where are we going?" he asked.

"Let's go up to Point Lookout," Kate suggested.

"Good idea," Dan said. "On the way we can take Pete through the Indian village, past Skull Cave, and by the two cemeteries."

"You're not saying all this just to scare me out of my wits, are you?" Pete muttered. "Because if you are, it's too late. This horse has already done that. I've been wit-less for several minutes, now."

"No, honest, Pete," Dan laughed. "We just want you to get an idea of all the stuff that's here on the Island."

The four bounced easily in their saddles as the horses cantered a quarter of a mile up Harrisonville Road. Pete slowly was gaining confidence when, up ahead, a man and woman on a tandem bike and two children on small bicycles approached them. Pete saw that the little boy wasn't looking ahead as he careened down the hill weaving from side to side.

"Look out," Pete yelled.

The boy glanced up and his eyes got as big as cannon balls. He was heading straight for Pete. The boy screamed as he locked his brakes. Chester rose up on his hind feet just as the boy and his bike slid past him. The big Morgan came down with all four hooves in high gear.

"Whoa!" Pete shrieked, grabbing the saddle horn. Chester raced frantically along Harrisonville Road. Up ahead, a bronze-skinned boy with long, black hair took one look, dropped an armload of kindling, and darted toward Pete. With an incredibly athletic leap, the young Indian sprang up and landed across Chester's withers bringing the horse to a stop. Kate, Dan, and Eddie tore up from behind at a full gallop.

The four horses gathered in the middle of the Indian village with a crowd of people gaping at Pete.

"Are you okay?" the Indian boy asked him.

Pete sat stiff in the saddle, his face as white as a bass's belly. "Yeah, I guess. But you can bet I wouldn't have been if you hadn't stopped this horse. Thanks. You saved my life."

"Naw, he would have stopped sooner or later," the boy said, slipping down from Chester's neck.

"See," Dan said, "I told you you'd be wanting to race us before long. I just didn't expect it so soon."

"Yeah, and never again either," Pete breathed.

"There, now that you've survived the worst thing that can happen," Kate said, moving her horse ahead as the crowd dispersed, "I guess we can get on with our ride. Maybe you should let one of us lead the way from now on."

"No arguments there," Pete said, managing a weak smile.

"Okay, here we go," Kate continued. "First, it's off to Skull Cave. Now, the neat thing about Skull Cave is that Alexander Henry hid there from the Indians after escaping the massacre at Fort Michilimackinac on the mainland. His Indian friend, Wawatam, brought him here to the Island, but when Wawatam saw how angry the other Ojibways were against British people, he told Henry that he'd better hide. Wawatam took Henry up into the woods and they found this cave. Henry slept the night here but when daylight came, he looked around and found he'd been sleeping on hundreds of human skeletons. To this day nobody knows where those bones came from."

"Let's go inside," Eddie said as the four stood with their horses at the cave opening. "There are still lots of bones way back in there."

"Skeletons, eh?" Pete mumbled. "Dead people, right? I don't think so. You know, I'm just getting the hang of riding. What say we just move along? We wouldn't want to hold your aunt and uncle up from their lunch."

"Okay," Dan laughed as he slid easily from his horse. "But for the next place, you'll have to dismount. It's the cemetery. It's unlucky to ride past a burial ground."

"Unlucky?" Pete said raising his eyebrows. "You mean something really bad might happen if I don't get off this horse? Let me just take a moment to review the past month for you. I've been shot at, driven over, chased, and, oh yes, almost drowned in so many new and interesting ways that I'm losing count. Now, you say that if I don't get off this horse right now I might have some bad luck?"

"You don't always have bad luck," Kate reminded him. "You made a lucky catch in that softball game."

"That was not luck," Pete said, rising up in the saddle. "That was skill. Getting whacked by a boom, running into a dock, riding a runaway horse—THAT's luck. And GOOD luck, it's not," Pete countered. "But, okay, if it makes you nervous, I'll get off the horse." Pete slipped his right foot out of the stirrup and swung his leg over Chester's immense haunches. As he stretched to place his right foot on the ground, his left foot got caught up in the stirrup. Pete flopped backwards onto the road, his leg high in the air and his shoulders dragging along in the dusty trail. Chester, still apparently miffed over the bicycle incident, began to walk along, dragging Pete at his side.

Kate ran from her horse and grabbed Chester's reins. "Whoa," she called out and Chester stopped.

Pete wriggled his left foot out of the stirrup and fell the rest of the way to the ground. "You know what?" Pete said, lying in the dirt, "I think I have a pretty good idea of how to get home. Sort of back that way, right?" He hopped up on his feet and took two steps along the road.

"No, it's the other way," Dan laughed. "Besides, you can't walk all the way home. Come on, you've been doing great. Here. I'll give you a hand."

Pete turned to his friends. "Okay, I'll give it one more shot. But if I get creamed this time, I'm going to spend the rest of this trip on your aunt and uncle's front porch. Look, I'm not one to just sit around reading books, but if you force me, by golly, I'll do it. Tell me, really, what's your idea of a vacation? I thought we were coming here for some fun. Being dragged around Mackinac Island by a horse is not my idea of a great time."

"All right," Dan said. "I promise, the rest of the trip will be peaceful. Okay?"

Pete held his head and rubbed his eyes. "Okay."

"All right, then. I'll help you get back up. We'll go real slow and stay only on the easiest trails," Dan promised.

Pete walked back to his horse. "All right," Pete said turning to Dan. "But if I'm going horseback riding, I want to learn how to get up all by myself. What's the trick?"

"That's the spirit," Dan said. "Okay, put your left foot in the stirrup, grab the horn, and think `spring.' Bounce once or twice, and jump."

Pete did and swung his leg over the big Morgan.

"Great!" Kate applauded. "Way to go, Pete! Now, you've really got it. We can go anywhere."

"Terrific," Pete replied. "What say we just ease our way back to the barn?"

"Just one more place," Kate said anxiously. "Follow me."

She lit out north and by the time the boys had caught up to her, she was starting down a trail near the West Bluff.

"This is Pontiac's Lookout," Kate called back to Pete. She guided her horse along a trail and told him about how Pontiac was one of the Indian leaders against the British and how the Indians attacked Fort Michilimackinac. She explained how Alexander Henry, the British trader, hid in a loft and watched as the Indians scalped the English soldiers and drank their blood.

Pete kept close to Kate listening to the story and didn't notice how narrow the trail had become or how close it was to the cliff. When the trail widened, Kate turned to face him.

"And now you've just done the hardest horse trail on Mackinac Island," Kate smiled.

"What?" Pete said. He glanced back behind him

and nearly fainted. It was a sheer drop-off into Lake Huron from about two hundred feet up on the bluff. "Holy cow! We just went through that?"

"Yep," Eddie said, himself relieved that he'd made Pontiac's Lookout safely. "I've only tried that once myself. You're a pro, Pete."

"Hear, hear!" Dan said. "Way to go, Pete."

"Race you home!" Pete laughed.

"Edna Fisher's cottage had the most spectacular view . . ."

CHAPTER 9
DINNER AT THE ANNEX

"Time to get ready, Pete," Dan called into Pete's bedroom.

For a vacation, everyone seems mighty anxious to keep me moving, Pete thought. *And after that horse ride my butt needs a break.*

Pete had come back from horseback riding, eaten lunch, gone upstairs to stretch out for just a second, and crashed.

"Okay, what's next, skydiving?" Pete mumbled, his face still firmly embedded in the goose down mattress.

"No, dinner," Dan replied.

"Already? We just had lunch."

"That was five hours ago," Dan said, opening Pete's door. "It's six o'clock. I guess when you take a snooze, you don't mess around, do you?"

"There might be some things I'm not real good at," Pete said coming to the door, "but with a little training, I could be a world-class napper."

"Well, you'd better get rolling or we'll be late," Dan laughed. "We're taking the carriage to the Annex in twenty minutes."

———

Charles, the Anderson's chauffeur, sat atop the driver's seat in the *vis-a-vis* style carriage while the four dinner guests rode in its fancy, velvet-seated coach. Pete and Kate sat in back facing Dan and Eddie as the two-horse team wended its way north along West Bluff Road and then into a dense forest. They emerged in a sun-filled meadow riding a narrow path through a community of elegant cottages. The lush, green park, about twice the size of a football field, smelled of freshly mown grass. A large croquet course was set up, and four long, wooden mallets leaned against a sideline bench. The players had evidently taken a dinner break and would resume their match later.

The carriage continued along the path to the largest of all the summer homes. Its front entrance faced the commons, but Pete could tell that the back was perched right out over the West Bluff.

"Whoa," Charles called to his team. Pete's eyes darted anxiously to the outside. He made a move for the door.

"Wait, Pete, " Kate said. "We have to let Charles open the latch."

Before Pete could ask, "What for?" the driver had sprung from his seat and was standing at the side of the carriage. He opened the door and, bowing deeply, extended his arm toward Edna Fisher's cottage gate. Pete bolted up but, once again, he was halted, this time by Dan. Kate then took Charles' hand and stepped gracefully from the carriage. She was followed in turn by each of the three boys.

Edna Fisher greeted her guests and opened the wide gate of her white, picket fence. She smiled broadly, but her eyes revealed even more tension than when she had been aboard the *Sea Gal.*

"Welcome, everyone. I'm so glad you could come," she smiled wearily. "That is a lovely carriage and team you have. If your driver would like, he could bring his rig to my barn while we dine. Oh, there I go, I'm so sorry, I haven't introduced myself to your friends. I'm Edna Fisher," she smiled first to Kate, and then to Dan and Eddie.

"This is Kate Hinken and her twin brother, Dan," Pete said. "They're the niece and nephew of George and Nancy Anderson who have a summer home on the West Bluff. That's where we're staying. And this is Eddie Terkel, our neighbor in the Les Cheneaux Islands." Pete had broken into a nervous sweat. He'd never introduced anyone formally before, and he was sure he'd done it all wrong. He glanced over at Kate and she winked her approval.

Edna opened the gate, smiled, and said, "Please excuse the grounds. There has been some vandalism lately. I'm trying to get to the bottom of it, but it seems someone is bent on destroying everything I own."

Pete looked to his left and then to his right. Piles of black dirt and deep holes pocked her lawn.

"What happened?" Pete asked.

"I wish I could tell you," Miss Fisher replied. "Every time I leave for any time at all, something else is ruined."

"How long has this been going on?" Kate asked.

"It started about two weeks ago. A pane of glass was shattered in the back door. I thought it must have been an accident. We've never had anything broken in all my years. It looked as if a burglar had tried to break in, except I never lock the door. Then other things began to happen."

"No one from your staff has ever seen anything?" Kate asked.

The old lady smiled wryly, "Staff?" she said. "Dear, I haven't needed a staff in years. Since my father died thirty-seven years ago, there's been no need for any extra help. I care for my horse and he is, indeed, a blessing.

47

We enjoy our days together going for long rides. Now, I'm afraid to leave the grounds for fear something else will happen.Well, enough of my problems. This is to be an evening of fun. I've planned a lovely dinner. Two friends of mine, local Indians, bring fresh fish when they have extra. Today, they caught two beautiful whitefish. I think whitefish are the tastiest of all the Great Lakes' fish. They used to be so plentiful in the Straits waters, but now they're very scarce. Oh, there I go, rambling on again. Do come in, and please ask your driver to join us."

"I'm afraid he can't," Dan said. "His services will be needed by my aunt and uncle this evening. They're going out to Stonecliff later on. We're to call from here when we're finished with our visit." Dan nodded to Charles, and the driver boarded the carriage. He completed the circle around the Annex and left by the same path into the woods that had brought him there.

The four guests followed their hostess along the fieldstone walk and through the front door. "Please, again I must beg your pardon," Edna Fisher said, "the condition of the house, too, is shocking. Everything has occurred so suddenly. Nothing like this has ever happened before. I don't live extravagantly, but with the trust set up by my father, I've never wanted for anything."

As they passed through the hallway, the four couldn't help noticing the obvious acts of destruction along the way. A hole had been beaten into the plaster wall. A picture had been smashed, a window pane broken, a floorboard from a small room had been wrenched from its place and thrown aside.

"I've cleaned the broken vases, figurines, and such, but I've yet to find a handyman to repair the walls and floor. Please, pay it no mind. The dining room is just ahead. I owe you all so much for saving my boat. I don't know what I'd have done if the *Sea Gal* had broken loose and smashed on the rocks yesterday. Its lines would surely have snapped if Pete hadn't stepped in and offered his help. The *Sea Gal* was a gift from my father. So, you see, it's more than just a boat. It means everything to me." The four followed Miss Fisher into a large room with a long, dining table. There were chairs enough to seat a dozen people. "Here," Edna said, "I've prepared some *hors d'oeuvres*. I'll just finish in the kitchen and then we'll have dinner."

"Can we help?" Pete asked.

"If you'd like," Edna replied. "Yes, that would be nice. We could visit while we work. I may have gotten myself in over my head tonight. You see, I haven't entertained in ages. And when I returned here from the harbor yesterday and saw what had happened to the front lawn, well, I must confess, if I'd have known how to reach you, I would probably have canceled our plans for tonight. But now I'm glad I couldn't. Having someone to talk to besides my nephew has already done my spirits a world of good."

"Your nephew?" Kate asked.

"Yes," Edna said, turning to Kate. "I've recently become guardian to my dear sister Alexa's only child, Ronald. Alexa lived with her husband, Edward Sawyer, on Bois Blanc Island. Edward died in a tragic accident twenty-five years ago. Alexa and Ronald lived there ever since, never leaving Bois Blanc even once. I would visit her in her little cabin every year in July, but she never came here. And now, even she is gone," Edna said, shaking her head.

"Ronald, who, I'm afraid, is somewhat mentally retarded, has come to stay with me. He's not doing very well, adjusting to his new surroundings. Mackinac Island is nothing like the backwoods of Bois Blanc. Since he's been here, he's spent most of his time away from my cottage. Right now, he's probably in town at the pool hall. He tries so hard to act grown up that I'm afraid he's fallen in with a rather unsavory group of men. Gamblers and drinkers and such."

"Could he be causing all the damage around here?" Dan asked.

"Oh, heavens, no," Edna said with a nervous laugh. "He wouldn't do that. No, I'm sure it's not Ronald, but I'm afraid I haven't any idea who it could be. Tourists, maybe. Summer employees. I don't know."

"Well," Eddie interrupted, "it looks like someone's trying to find something. Is anything hidden around here?"

"No, there's nothing here," Edna Fisher said. "Well," she said, raising her head. "There is an old myth about a hidden treasure. But that's all it is—a legend. You see, my father, Lemuel Fisher, was a Civil War general. After the war, the government gave him most of Bois Blanc Island as a compensation for his service to his country. He built a cabin and stayed there for a year writing his memoirs, but then he got tired of that and began to visit Mackinac Island. Here, he met my mother who was spending the summer with the Stuart family. They fell in love at first sight and soon were married. He bought this property and had this house built up here in the Annex.

"Then, when I was six, only three years after my sister was born, my mother died. After that, my father did practically nothing but write poetry—whimsical rhymes, mainly." Edna sat back in her chair. "My, how he missed my mother—and loved this island," she mused, staring into the distance. She shook her head, snapping herself from her reverie. "Soon after Mother died, he sold his Bois Blanc property. That's where the myth began, I guess. Everyone said that he made a fortune from it and turned all the earnings into gold coins. Then they say he stashed them in large, silver canisters. Some say he sealed and buried them on Bois Blanc Island while others think he hid them here on Mackinac. People have searched for those cans for over thirty years, but none have ever been discovered. Of course, if a person found one, he wouldn't likely announce it, would he?

"But I think," Edna continued, "like so many other myths, it's simply a fanciful story. Imaginative tales of hidden fortune are much more exciting than the simple truth, don't you agree? People love such things. I, myself, don't believe he ever had even one gold coin. We lived very modestly here in the Annex supported entirely by my father's government pension.

"It's tragic, but it's only because of that legend that my sister's husband died. Once he heard about the silver canisters, he became obsessed with finding them. He often left Alexa and Ronald alone for days in their Bois Blanc cabin while he wandered about the woods. One summer day, twenty-five years ago, he went on what he called, a gold hunt. Ronald was only nine years old. When Ed didn't come home for three nights, Ronald, who had stayed at his mother's side throughout his father's absence, went into the woods to find him.

"It wasn't long before he came upon a campsite. There, he found his father's tent torn to shreds. Nearby, in a pool of dried, black blood, he discovered what was left of his father. Only a skull and a few bones remained. Apparently, he'd been killed by a bear or a pack of wolves. What was left of him after that was consumed by raccoons, large birds, and Lord knows what other woodland creatures. Ronald was dumbstruck and went into shock. He roamed about, terrified of being caught by the same animals that had killed his father. He became lost in the woods, and for two days stumbled around before finding his way back to his house. When he found his mother he pulled her by the hand to his father's remains. He didn't speak to anyone for over a year. Not one word.

"From that day to this, Ronald has never been completely well, mentally. Alexa, herself in deep remorse, did little to help Ronald. I pleaded with her to let him stay with me, at least for a while, but she refused."

Edna looked up at her stunned guests. "Oh, dear," she sighed, "I'm afraid I've turned this lovely occasion into a cry session. Enough of me. I want to learn all about you," she smiled, wiping her eyes. "Let's get into the kitchen and whip up dinner."

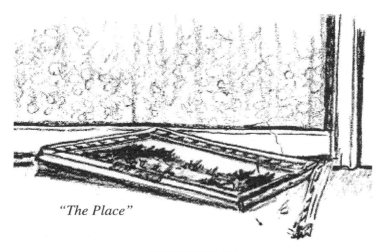

"The Place"

CHAPTER 10
THE POEM

All four followed Edna Fisher through a swinging door. Surprisingly, nothing was out of place in the large kitchen. All five got to work. In minutes they were chattering about the storm and their stay so far on the Island. They were just carrying the trays of food into the dining room when the front door slammed. A clashing and clattering shook the house and the rumbling of footsteps charged up the wide stairway to the second floor. The four friends glanced at each other and then at Edna. She had turned a ghostly white. Edna hurried into the front hallway. Her guests followed.

"Ronald," she called up the stairs. "Is that you?"

"Yes, Aunt Edna," came a small voice.

"Oh, gracious," she sighed, "you must be more careful. I'm afraid something has broken."

"I'm sorry," Ronald said. "I was in a hurry to get to the bathroom. I didn't want to have an accident."

Edna turned from the stairway, shaking her head. "I declare," she said, "it's like having a child around. He can be so sweet sometimes. And others . . ." She turned and again called up the stairs. "We have dinner guests, Ronald. Would you like to meet them?"

"Okay," Ronald replied meekly.

"I'm sure I heard something break. I must see what fell," Edna said. She entered a large study next to the front entrance. There, an oil painting of a peaceful, wooded glen lay on the floor. A metal tab on the base of the frame read, "The Place."

"Oh, dear," Edna said with a sigh. "It's my father's favorite piece of art. He told me once that it was more valuable than anything else in the house. It seems he was wrong about that, too. After he passed away, Alexa and I had it appraised. It was almost worthless. Still, it was his favorite, so I should have it repaired."

Edna picked the canvas away from the frame and a yellowed envelope slid to the floor. "What's this?" she said, picking it up. She blinked and then handed it to Pete. "I don't have my glasses, Peter, could you read it?"

"Sure," he said, opening the sealed folder. He adjusted the paper to get the best light. "It's kind of scribbly. It looks like a poem—two lines to a stanza and four—no, five verses."

"Can you tell who signed it?" Edna asked.

Pete looked again. "`L. Fisher,' it says. `June 21, 1915.'"

"My word! That's the month before he died," Edna gasped. "Oh, but I'm sure it's just another of his rhymes to Mackinac Island. I can't imagine how he could have wasted so much time. There, now, our food is getting cold. Maybe we'll read it after dessert. Come, let's sit down."

———

After dinner, Kate asked Edna about the poem.

"All right," Edna smiled. "But I can tell you what it's about without even looking at it. My father loved to wander about the Island. I believe he wrote a poem about every rock and tree here. He had most of them published a few years before he died, but I doubt if a copy exists, or that anyone alive has ever read it. I am a little surprised at this one, though. You said it has five stanzas, Pete?"

"Yup," he said glancing back at it. "Two lines to a verse."

Edna scanned it. "That is odd. Except for a few three-stanza rhymes, all the rest were only two verses long. Let's see if we can read it. Pete, you try."

Pete adjusted the paper for the best light. "Okay," he said squinting. "Here goes:

'Illini Route, Fort Holmes Flag,
Marquette Park, Langlade Craig.

Haldimand Bay, Griffin Cove,
Hennepin Point, Sinclair Grove.

Old Fort Garden, Forest King,
Tom Scott's Cave, Dwightwood Spring.

Wawashkamo Links, Breakwater West,
Carver Pond, Schoolcraft Rest.

Charlevoix Heights, Turtle Back,
Baraga View, Northeast Crack.'

"That's it," Pete said, turning it over and checking the back.

"Why, it's just a bunch of place names," Edna said. "They rhyme and the meter is like the rest of his poems, but that's all they are—Mackinac Island sites. Are you sure there's not another line? No moral, or something?"

"Nope," Pete said, looking it over once again. "That's it."

"Well, that's a first," Edna conceded. "I . . ." She stopped suddenly. Something was scratching softly at the wall. She held up a hand for everyone to listen.

"Ronald," she said. "Is that you?"

"Yes, Aunt Edna," a trembling voice responded from the adjoining room.

Edna breathed a sigh of relief. "Come in, Ronald," she said kindly. "I'd like you to meet my guests."

A shuffling of footsteps came along the hallway and soon the strangest man Pete had ever seen in all his life walked into the dining room. It was hard to say exactly, but he could have been thirty or forty years old. He had closely cropped brown hair with small patches of white throughout. He wore the sweet, innocent countenance of a boy, but had the heavy, thick muscles of a man. He was roundish, hunched over, and short, no more than five foot, four inches tall, and built rather like an oak stump. He had short arms and squat legs and moved a little like an overgrown mouse.

His stubby fingers were grimy, dirt forced deep under the nails as though he'd been playing marbles all day. The knees of his trousers, too, were torn and smudged with soil. His face was contorted into the mixed expressions of disorientation, innocence, and irresolute sadness. He looked truly bewildered. He certainly did not seem to be the vicious, mean-spirited person that Pete had pictured from the librarian's description.

Could this child-like, simple man standing before him be part of an act? Or could he be a raging lunatic capable of sinister deeds in one moment and acts of love and devotion at the flip of a switch? He'd heard of such people. It was clear, however, that all was not right with Ronald Sawyer. Pete was anxious to hear him speak and was disappointed when he didn't.

"Would you like to sit with us, Ronald?" Edna asked.

He nodded and glanced nervously from face to face of the four teenagers before him. He took a seat at the end of the long, dining room table and sat quietly, intensely monitoring every action of those before him.

"We were just reading one of your Grandfather Lemuel's poems, Ronald," Edna said. "Would you like to listen along with us?"

"No," Ronald said, his face clouding into a scowl. "I already heard it." He pushed his chair back and stood up. "I want it," he growled.

"This isn't going to work," Edna said to her guests. "I'm afraid he's going into one of his possessive moods. He can be very disruptive. Perhaps we should call it an evening. I'm sorry it had to end this way. Pete, I'd like you to keep this poem as a gift of appreciation for all you did yesterday at the dock."

"I couldn't take that," Pete said. "It's your father's last poem."

"I know," Edna stiffened. "But if I've learned anything about Ronald, it is that once he wants something, he'll try any means to get it. If I keep it here," Edna said, returning the parchment to its envelope, "it will be ruined. Please, take it. Perhaps you and your friends can use it as a travel guide following it around the Island as my father must have done when he wrote it. Yes. It would be as if you were walking in his footsteps. My father would have liked that."

"Well, that does sound like fun," Pete said. He glanced toward Ronald who could barely control his rage. "Maybe you'd better call for Charles to come, Dan," Pete added.

Edna showed Dan to the black, candlestick telephone in the front hall. In minutes, the Anderson carriage swept into the Annex and up to the Fisher home.

"Thank you for coming," Edna waved as the four boarded the carriage. "Please, visit again soon. You must tell me how you do with Father's poem."

The four waved and Charles signaled the team to move ahead.

Pete and Kate sat in the back of the *vis-a-vis* carriage looking forward while Dan and Eddie sat facing them looking out through the small, back window. It was almost dark, even in the open courtyard of the Annex, but when the carriage made its way into the forest, night closed in quickly. The team clomped along the winding inland road and then out into the moonlight as it approached the west bluff.

"Ronald's following us," Dan said calmly as the carriage come out of the woods. "I wasn't sure at first—just a feeling—but now I'm positive."

"How do you know that?" Eddie asked. "You wouldn't be setting us up for a night of ghost stories, would you?"

"Look for yourself," Dan said, pointing to a large maple tree behind them. "In a second you'll see him run from there to another hiding place. He's staying just close enough to keep us in sight."

Pete and Kate swung around and all four pressed their faces to the small, rear window of the carriage. A ray of moonlight caught the form of a ball-shaped figure as it moved from behind the maple tree and scurried along the road toward them. It stopped behind a white, picket fence sixty feet away.

"Okay, Dick Tracy," Eddie said, turning to Dan, "but why?"

"Maybe Ronald Sawyer would like to tell us some of his ghost stories," Kate said with a wry smile.

"I hope not," Pete said. "I wouldn't sleep for a month."

"I doubt that," Eddie laughed. "I've never met any-one who could nod off in mid-stride like you do."

The carriage turned onto the service path behind the West Bluff cottages. Charles stopped at the back of the Anderson's residence. The four piled out, Dan watching in the direction they had come.

"There he goes," Dan said, "back down the road. He knows where we live, and now he's going back to the Annex."

"I hope he stays there," Pete said. "He gives me the creeps." Pete carried General Fisher's poem as he fol-lowed Kate inside.

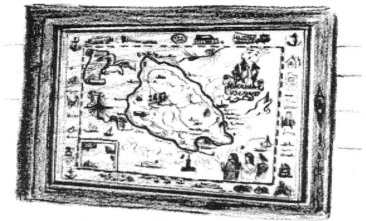

"I see some of the places already."

CHAPTER 11
DAY 4 EXPLORATION

"We've got the whole day to do anything we want," Kate said as the four leaned over the breakfast table filled with fruits and pastries.

"I say we do what Edna Fisher said," Eddie suggested, picking out a kiwi fruit. "Let's take the poem around to all the places General Fisher wrote about."

"We could do the ones in town this morning," Dan added, "and the others this afternoon."

"The paper looks kind of flimsy," Pete said, unfolding it. "Do you think we should take it with us?"

"Sure," Dan said, "I've got just the thing to carry it in. Uncle George lets us use his Civil War letter pouch whenever we take party invitations to his friends. It would be perfect for this."

"Let me see the poem, Pete," Kate said. "When you read it last night, there were places I'd never heard of."

"Like Illini Route and Sinclair Grove," Dan said, looking over Pete's shoulder. "Maybe Aunt and Uncle can tell us where these places are. 'Charlevoix Heights, Schoolcraft

Rest, Baraga View'—I wonder if the General wasn't making these up," he added with a laugh.

"Aunt and Uncle haven't come downstairs yet," Kate said. "I say we just head out to the library. Miss Martin probably knows where all these places are right off the top of her head. If she doesn't, at least she'd know of a book or something where we could find them."

"Let's roll," Eddie said, pushing his chair back. "We'll get the bikes and go into town before the streets get too busy."

———

"Thanks, Miss Martin," Kate said as the four stood in front of a faded, three-foot by four-foot wall map of Mackinac Island. "This is great. I see some of the places in the poem already."

"Poem?" Mrs. Martin smiled. "Do you have a poem about Mackinac Island?"

"Yes," Kate said, removing the envelope from the courier bag. "We think it's Lemuel Fisher's last one. See, it's dated just a month before he died. We found it last night at Edna Fisher's place. She gave it to Pete to use as a guide to the Island."

"The only trouble," Dan added, "is that we've never heard of most of the places."

Kate laid the paper on the table in front of the wall map. Miss Martin studied it intensely.

"There's another one," Eddie said, pointing to a spot on the map. "Griffin Cove. They sure are all over the place."

"What do those numbers mean on your map, Miss Martin?" Kate asked. "There are almost as many numbers as there are names."

"Oh, they're probably just minor points that the mapmaker didn't have room to spell out on the paper," the librarian explained.

"Maybe," Dan said slowly. "But this map seems to be big enough to write practically anything on it. It's like it was copied from a smaller map, maybe in a book or something."

"Miss Martin," Kate said, turning to the librarian, "do you know of any book like that?"

"I'm not aware of any," Hazel Martin answered. She glanced at her watch. "Well, kids, I have to close the library for a while. There's a meeting I must attend. If you'd like to leave your things here until I come back, I'm sure they'll be safe."

"Okay," Kate said, "we'll come back after lunch. There must be something that tells where these places are."

"I'll look in the archives when I return," the librarian said, "but I'm afraid I must go now. You're welcome to leave your things here," she repeated.

"We'd better take the poem with us," Pete said. "I'd hate to have something happen to it, like if Ronald came along and stole it, or something."

"Yes, yes," Miss Martin agreed. "That would be tragic. Let me just take a moment to mark some of the names on a slip of paper. I'll check them out as soon as my meeting is over."

She scribbled on a legal pad and turned to leave. "Okay, I'll see what I can find. Come back after lunch."

"Schoolcraft Rest looks out into the harbor."

CHAPTER 12
THE BOOK

"Well timed, kids," Nancy Anderson said as Dan led the four house guests into the living room. "Run upstairs and change. We're going on a picnic. Zachary has the food just about ready."

Soon the four had scrubbed and returned to the living room. Chef Zachary had prepared a trunk loaded with food, and Mr. Anderson was holding a large wicker basket by the front door. Pete followed Kate outside and down the stairs to the carriage. Charles, the chauffeur, and Chef Zachary loaded everything aboard as Mr. and Mrs. Anderson and their four guests seated themselves in the coach. Zachary finished packing the trunk and joined Charles in the driver's seat.

"To Ann's Tablet," George Anderson called up to Charles, and they were off.

In minutes they had covered the short distance behind Fort Mackinac and slowed to a stop at a place in the woods. Pete looked around. There didn't seem to be any reason to be getting out here. Nonetheless, everyone was following Mr. Anderson along a walking path into the woods. When Pete looked up he saw a three-foot by four-foot, solid bronze plaque laying atop an even larger flat rock. Beyond it was a circle of stone benches set up perfectly for songfests or picnics. Pete took another step and saw a clearing ahead. He walked to the cliff's edge and stood overlooking Marquette Park and Mackinac Harbor.

"Pretty neat, eh?" Kate said, coming up from behind. "Follow me. You're not going to believe this." She took Pete's hand and they headed up a hill. She stopped at the edge of the cliff. "Practically no one knows about this place," she said. There at their feet in front of them was Fort Mackinac, the village, Round Island light, Round Island, Bois Blanc, the harbor, the park, St. Anne's Church, Mission Point—everything.

"Wow," Pete said. "How come nobody knows about it?"

"Beats me," Kate answered. "But it's my favorite place on the whole island. Let's get back before Dan and Eddie eat everything."

Chef Zachary and Charles were busy unpacking the food while George Anderson was opening the wicker basket. It was filled with silverware, china cups, saucers, and plates. Last, he pulled out a silver tea service with a small kerosene burner. Soon Chef Zachary was serving trays of sandwiches, croissants, and biscuits with a proper cup of tea for everyone.

"How did the morning go?" George Anderson asked.

"It was great," Kate said. "We went to the library. Last night Edna Fisher gave Pete a poem that her father had written just before he died. It was really strange. It named a whole bunch of Mackinac Island places that we've never heard of. We found out where some of them are at the library, but there were just as many that we

64

couldn't find. Here, look at this. Maybe you know where some of them are."

Kate opened the envelope and handed the poem to Mr. Anderson.

"Well, I know where this one is," George Anderson said. "Schoolcraft Rest. It's a stopping place on the path from the park below us up here to the bluff."

"I've heard about Henry Schoolcraft," Mrs. Anderson said. "He was an Indian agent. I remember reading about him in a large, blue book at the library years ago. Now that I think of it, that book had a folding map in it with lots of places I'd never heard of. The librarian at the time said that it was a very rare book. It must still be there."

"Why don't you ask Miss Martin about that?" Mr. Anderson suggested. "Maybe she has it but just didn't think about it this morning."

"Could be," Dan nodded.

"It's not that big a deal," Eddie said. "We're just doing it for fun. It's not like it's the Rosetta Stone or something that will solve any big mystery."

"What's the Rosetta Stone," Pete asked.

"It's an ancient stone tablet that archaeologists used to figure out what all the Egyptian tombs had written on them," Eddie said. "All I'm saying is that this book that Aunt Nancy is talking about isn't going to solve any big secrets, so let's not worry about it."

"Still, it would be fun to find all of the places in the poem," Kate said.

"Yes, if only to tell Edna Fisher that we did it," Dan added.

"Well," Pete said, "you don't have to go to all that trouble just to show me around."

"Okay," Kate agreed. "But after our picnic, let's at least go back to the library and ask Miss Martin about the book."

A light breeze rustled the birch leaves high over the quiet setting as everyone finished lunch. Charles and Zachary tidied the area, and soon the horses were clomping along the dirt road back to the West Bluff.

———

"Could we see that map again, Miss Martin?" Dan asked.

"Certainly," the librarian said with a smile. "What do you hope to find?"

"I don't know," he replied, following her to the reference area. "Maybe there's something on it that tells what it's taken from. Aunt Nancy says she remembers an old, blue book that had some maps of the Island in it."

"There," Kate pointed to the upper right hand corner of the wall map. "'Mapped by Morgan H. Wright, E.M., Marquette, Mich. expressly for *Historic Mackinac*, copyrighted by Edwin O. Wood, 1915.' That must be the name of the book Aunt Nancy remembers, *Historic Mackinac*."

"Have you ever heard of that, Miss Martin?" Dan asked.

"No, I don't think so," she replied, turning and looking at the three shelves reserved for Mackinac Island history. "It would be here if it were anywhere, though."

"This is odd," Dan said scanning the reference area. "Of these three shelves, only the middle one isn't full. There's a space here where the books have fallen over." He straightened them leaving about a four-inch gap. "How long has the shelf been like that?" he asked.

"I guess I've never noticed it," Miss Martin said. "But I suppose you're right. If a two-volume set entitled, 'Historic Mackinac,' would have been here, that's where it would go."

"Two volumes?" Dan asked. "Aunt Nancy didn't say that it had two volumes."

"Oh, I'm just guessing," Miss Martin said, turning away. "If it's that large a space, it probably was done in two volumes."

"Well," Eddie said, "it's no big deal. We have plenty we can do while we're here without spending all our time tracking down some old book. Let's hit the trail."

"Wait a minute, Eddie," Kate said. "We've got to mark the places in the poem on our trail map."

"If it's all right with you," the librarian said, "I'd like to write that poem down. It would be horrible if something happened to the only copy of a Lemuel Fisher poem—even if it is just the whimsy of an old eccentric."

"Go ahead, Miss Martin," Pete said. "Just as long as I can keep the real one. I'm going to frame it and hang it at the cottage when I get back to the Snows."

Both Eddie and Miss Martin got busy and finished in a few minutes.

"Let's take our bikes to the places that we know about," Dan said. "At least we can go to half of them, even if we don't know much about them."

"Okay," Eddie said, folding the map.

"Lead on, captain," Dan bowed to his friend and the four hurried outside.

"This was once the favorite landing place for Indian tribes."

CHAPTER 13
THE TRAIL

"What's first?" Kate asked.

"Well, mates," Eddie squinted in the sunlight, "it appears that about half the places are right along the shore."

"We could do a Oami," Dan said.

"A wommy?" Pete asked. "It sounds Indian. This isn't going to get me killed, is it?"

"No, Pete," Dan laughed, hopping on this bike. "A Oami is short for 'Once around Mackinac Island.'"

"That'll take forever," Pete said, looking over Eddie's shoulder at all the red marks on the map.

"We can quit when we want to," Dan said. "Let's start at the west breakwall."

In less than a minute the four had rolled down the hill from the library to the point next to the Iroquois Hotel. They came to a sign which Kate read aloud as the others watched a freighter pass no more than a hundred yards in front of them. "'This point was once the favorite landing place for Indian tribes from all over the Great Lakes,'" Kate recited. "'The breakwater was constructed to protect the harbor from the prevailing southwesterly winds that once caused great damage in Haldimand Bay.' I love this spot," she added. "There's something so amazing about the ships from all over the Great Lakes passing so near. I'll bet Lemuel Fisher felt the same way when he chose this as one of the sites for his poem."

The warm, afternoon sun beat down on the teenagers. "Where to now, Eddie?" Kate asked.

"Griffin Cove," Eddie said, checking the map. "I can tell you a ton about that right now," he said, getting on his bike. "Not the place, exactly, but the name. The *Griffin* was the first boat other than a canoe to ever sail the Great Lakes. My dad named our sailboat after it. On its first trip LaSalle took it from Niagara Falls to Green Bay. He loaded it with pelts and sent it back to Niagara while he stayed in Green Bay to explore. That was the last time the *Griffin* was ever seen."

"What?" Pete laughed. "Your dad named his boat after a ship that went down on its first trip?"

"I never thought of it that way," Eddie said. "I think he did it because our island in the Snows is named after LaSalle. He and his pals did some pretty wild things. They were always risking their lives with the Indians. Even his own men were afraid that he would get them killed. LaSalle had a knack of staying just one step ahead of his enemies—except for the last time, of course. He was killed by his own men down in Texas."

"I guess this must be Griffin Cove," Dan said, bringing his bike to a stop. "What's next, Eddie."

"Look over there, Pete," Eddie said, pointing ahead. "That's Hennepin Point. Hennepin was one of LaSalle's buddies on the *Griffin*. He wrote a lot about their adventures and how hard it was to live back then."

"If life was so bad, why would anyone ever come here?" Pete asked.

"Probably because it was worse everywhere else," Dan said. "All the kings and queens back in Europe were always having wars, so either you had to fight in their armies or you had to work and pay taxes to pay for the men who did. Either way, it wasn't much fun. Plus, all the cities were crowded and dirty, and there were plagues and diseases everywhere. When they heard about all the open spaces and free land around here, it sounded pretty good. So they came. Once they got here they found out about the snakes and mosquitoes and Indians, but they made the best of it, anyway."

"Next is Dwightwood Spring," Eddie said.

The four hopped back on their bikes and rode two hundred yards along the shoreline until they pulled up to a rest area with two wooden benches. They went to a shelter where a bronze plaque was mounted on a stone wall. Dan read it aloud: "'This memorial, facing the rising sun, is dedicated and christened in memory of a charming, noble boy, Dwight Hulbert Wood, son of Hon. Edwin O. Wood of Flint, Michigan. Dwight sacrificed his life for his brother, August 12, 1905.'"

"I choke up every time I read that," Eddie said. "I always wonder what this kid did to save his brother's life."

"Me, too," Dan said. "But it's a great place for something like this. People bottle this water and send it all over the world. They say it's good for all sorts of sicknesses."

"Now, we'll have to go inland for the next stop," Eddie said, getting back on his bike.

In minutes the four were on their way to the top of the Island. "Right up ahead is Wawashkamo Links," Dan said. "Its name means, 'Crooked Trail,' because an Indian who was watching the first golfers saw that they were walking all over the place as they went from one flag to the next. I guess the duffers back then weren't any

70

straighter hitters than they are now," Dan said with a laugh. "It's also where the Battle of Mackinac Island took place. Right over there is where Major Holmes was killed."

"Well, I guess that's about it," Kate said. "We've been to all the places in the General's poem that are shown on the map."

"So far," Dan said, "I don't see what any of this has to do with a treasure."

"Me neither," Eddie agreed.

"Maybe if we find the rest of the places," Kate said, "something will jump out at us."

"Maybe we're trying too hard," Pete said. "Like the other night at the party, I was so full I didn't know what to eat next. It's like my dad says—sometimes a fish can't see the bait for all the worms."

"Now, check Fort Holmes Flag."

CHAPTER 14
DAY 5 THE LIGHT

"Pete, wake up," Dan said, shaking Pete's shoulder.

"Huh?" Pete rolled in his bed. "What time is it?"

"Three o'clock," Dan urged. "Come on. We need the poem."

"In the middle of the night?" Pete mumbled, sitting up.

"Yes, Pete. Hurry!" Kate whispered.

"Kate!" Pete almost shouted. He pulled the covers over himself. "What are you doing here?"

"Dan and I had a dream," she answered quickly. "It's weird, Pete, but whenever we have dreams with Indians in them, whatever happens next is a warning. If we wake up in time and put the dreams together, we can stop something terrible from happening. Tonight, I dreamed about Chief Pontiac standing at the bluff by the Annex. Then I saw General Fisher sitting at his desk writing on a map of Mackinac Island just like the one at the library. I woke up and knew I had to check it out with Dan right away. So, I ran to knock on Dan's door, but he was already coming to my door."

"My dream," Dan said quickly, "started with Chief Wawatam. Then it switched to General Fisher who was reading his poem about Mackinac Island out loud to the four of us. We were all in the dream. You, me, Eddie. . ."

"The first time this happened," Kate said, turning to go to the door, "was three summers ago. That night I dreamed about Chief Shab-wa-way, an old Les Cheneaux Indian. He was standing at the door of our boathouse and pointing inside."

"And my dream that night," Dan said, "began with another Snows Indian, Chief Tuskinaw. He was sitting before a huge bonfire. He faded out of the picture and a tremendous explosion woke me up. I jumped right out of my bed, and as soon as my feet hit the floor, I heard Kate scream in her room next to mine. I ran into her as she was coming through her door. She told me about her dream and, for some reason, I just took off down to the boat-house. I ran inside, and I found a rag smoldering inches away from a full tank of gas. If we'd have waited another minute, there'd have been one less boathouse in Cincinnati Row."

"The dreams we just had make us think that the General's poem and the Mackinac map have something very important to tell us," Kate said. "That poem we got from Edna must have more to it than just a list of Mackinac places. Hurry, Pete. Bring it downstairs."

Pete scrambled into his clothes and rushed two flights down to the dining room. Eddie, Dan, and Kate were already sitting at the long table, buzzing over the dreams.

"This is crazy," Pete said, standing behind Kate. "How could something you dream about in the middle of the night have anything to do with real life?"

"I don't understand it either," Dan said, "but Indians believe in them—that dreams are the doors to their souls.

Chiefs never did anything if they had a bad dream about it the night before."

"Look," Kate said. "This never happens to us back home, but up here, it's happened several times. Maybe it's because the air is so pure or the Indian spirits are so strong, I don't know, but if we don't figure this out fast, something awful could happen."

"Sounds like hocus-pocus to me," Pete yawned, "but here's the poem." He slid into a chair next to Kate. "I can't imagine what could be in it that we haven't thought of."

"There's got to be something," Kate said. "Let's go over it again." She opened the paper and laid it on the table.

"What do you make of this, Eddie?" Dan said, holding the poem in front him.

"Well," Eddie said, "it's different from any of the General's other poems. It's longer and doesn't have a moral or anything, but beyond that . . ." He shrugged his shoulders.

"Right," Kate agreed. "The others talked about only one or two places."

"How about you, Pete?" Dan said.

Pete shook his head. "If there's anything in there that the General had in mind when he wrote it, you'd think it would have happened a long time ago. This thing is over thirty-five years old, you know."

"Right," Dan said. "Maybe whatever clue he put in here was supposed to have been found thirty-five years ago, but wasn't. Anyway, here's what I make of it. When we read the poem two nights ago we'd never heard of most of these Mackinac Island places, right? So there didn't seem to be any pattern to it. But yesterday at the library we found that old map on the wall. We saw right away that it named several of the places in the General's poem. We thought we were on our way to finding all of them, but then we ran into a brick wall. Only half of the places were on the map. Now, here's where Kate's and my dreams come together. In mine, General Fisher kept fading in and out of focus—sort of like how some of the places are on the map and some aren't. Eddie, help me with this. As I read the names in the poem, check the map to see if they're listed."

"Okay, shoot," Eddie replied.

"Illini Route?" Dan asked, looking at the poem.

Eddie scoured the map he had copied from the library. "No," Eddie said, "it's not on here."

"Okay. Mark `Illini Route' as a `no.' Now, check Fort Holmes Flag," Dan continued.

"Yes," Eddie answered. "Right at the south wall of the fort.

"All right," Dan said. "That's a `yes.' How about Marquette Park?"

"Here it is," Eddie replied, pointing to the park near the harbor.

"Langlade Craig?"

"No."

"Haldimand Bay?"

"Well," Eddie said, "I know where it is, but it's not named on the map."

"Then, it's a `no,'" Dan said. "How about Griffin Cove?"

"Yes, it's up here by British Landing."

"That's enough. See the pattern?" Dan asked. "On every line of the poem one place is marked on the map and one isn't. Sometimes it's the first name on the line—sometimes it's the second. Now, remember the numbers on the map at the library? There were probably as many

75

numbers as there were names, right? Think about this for a minute. Suppose the places in the poem that aren't named are numbered? General Fisher, when he was writing the poem, knew that when the person matched the poem with all the places in the book that somehow they'd line up to form a clue. But they couldn't finish the puzzle unless they matched the NUMBERED places with the NAMED places on the map. The only person that could do that would be someone with both the General's poem and the old map!"

"That blue book Aunt Nancy told us about," Kate jumped up. "That has to hold the key! Maybe it is like the Rosetta Stone. We've got to find it."

"But where would it be?" Eddie asked. "It's not at the library. And Aunt Nancy said it was scarce years ago . . ."

Pete yawned and rubbed his eyes. "Strikes me," he said, "that if Lemuel Fisher wrote that poem with a puzzle in mind, he must have had the map and the book in front of him as he was writing it. He was probably sitting at a desk in his home up there at the Annex. Isn't that the same cottage Edna Fisher lives in now? Why don't we ask her tomorrow if she has a copy of the blue book?"

At the sound of Edna's name Kate stared at Dan. Dan just about came out of his seat. "Edna Fisher was in my dream, Kate. Was she in yours, too?" Dan asked.

"Not quite," Kate gasped. "But her cottage was. It was glowing—sort of like it was on fire."

"Then that's the message," Dan said, jumping to his feet. "Come on!"

"Where are you going?" Pete asked.

"To the barn to get the bikes," Dan answered. "Then up to the Annex."

76

Dan led the way past several Annex cottages.

CHAPTER 15
NIGHT LIGHT

"What if we get up there and nothing's going on?" Pete asked. "We'll look pretty stupid barging in on her at three in the morning."

"Let's worry about that when we get there," Dan said as the four crossed the horse path to the barn. "If nothing's happening, we'll just come back here."

"Shouldn't we tell your aunt and uncle?" Pete asked.

"If Dan's right," Eddie said, sliding the door open, "we don't have time for that. And I'll tell you what, Pete, I've seen Dan and Kate do this dream thing before. As crazy as it sounds, I don't doubt for a second what they say."

In minutes the four were cranking their pedals through the warm night. As they raced along the service path towards Hubbard's Annex the crescent moon flooded the clear sky with a soft, silver light. The branches of nearby birches waved over them in the breeze.

As he rode along Pete wondered why, practically every time he said anything to anyone, it got him into trouble. He made a mental note to keep his thoughts to himself in the future.

Dan led the way into the Annex past several cottages before pulling up in front of Edna Fisher's place. They dropped their bikes at the gate just as a small, hunched-over figure slid along Edna's porch and scurried into the shadows.

"Did you see that?" Dan whispered behind him.

"Sure did," Eddie answered. "It was either Ronald Sawyer or an overgrown groundhog."

The four gathered at the picket fence and looked into Edna Fisher's front yard. The moon was setting in a direct line behind the summer home casting a halo of glowing light all around it.

"This is too weird," Kate gasped. "It looks just like it did in my dream."

The house was silhouetted in the moonlight. All of the downstairs windows were as dark as the blackest night. One of the upstairs rooms, however, glimmered softly as though a night light were flickering in a corner. The four stared at the house waiting for something to happen.

Ten minutes passed. Nothing did.

"Well, it looks like a bum steer," Dan sighed. "I guess our dream-thing doesn't work every time, Kate."

"I guess not," Kate said. "I was so sure . . ."

As the four friends returned to their bicycles, Pete glanced back towards Edna's cottage.

"I don't know," Pete whispered to the others as they got on their bikes. "Is it just my eyes, or is that light upstairs getting brighter?"

"It's your eyes," Eddie yawned without turning. "Let's hit the hay."

Kate glanced back. She did a double-take and screamed, "Pete's right! Look!" she pointed.

"Holy cow!" Dan shrieked. "It's a fire. Come on!"

The four dropped their bikes and pushed open the

fence gate. They bolted across the lawn to the darkened front door. Eddie got there first and twisted the handle.

"It's locked," he said.

"Bang on it!" Dan yelled.

Eddie hit it with both fists. Nothing happened.

Kate gasped. She stumbled backwards and blanched in horror. "Oh, my word . . ." she murmured.

"What in the name of . . ." Dan breathed.

The moon and stars cast just enough light on the front door for the four teenagers to see the outline of a dozen dead squirrels, each hanging by its tail and forming a semicircle around the entrance to Edna Fisher's cottage.

"It wasn't like that when we came here for dinner, was it?" Pete asked.

"No, Pete," Dan whispered. "Believe me. It wasn't here two nights ago."

"Who could have done this?" Kate gasped.

"Probably the same person who started the fire upstairs," Dan exclaimed. "We've got to get inside. Eddie, bust it in!"

Eddie stepped back and lunged at the center of the circle of squirrels. The latch snapped and the door flew open.

"Kate, go find Miss Fisher," Dan yelled. "I'll get the fire."

The four raced inside and ran in different directions. Dan went upstairs. Kate followed Dan and opened the bedroom doors trying to find Edna. Eddie headed for the back of the cottage hoping to catch anyone trying to get away through the rear door. Pete had no real desire to go much farther than the front entrance. He stood in the hall and peeked into the dining room, kitchen, and den. No one was there, but he did find a light switch and turned it on. In seconds, all four met in the center of the downstairs hallway.

"What's going on?" a dazed Edna Fisher asked as she emerged with Kate from her bedroom. She was dressed in a long, white nightgown.

"We're not sure," Dan said hesitantly. "Has anyone found Ronald?" he asked.

"He's not upstairs," Kate replied.

"He's not down here," Eddie said.

"Doesn't he usually sleep here?" Dan asked Edna Fisher.

"Yes, of course," she said.

"Then it must have been Ronald we saw leaving when we got here," Dan said slowly.

Dan took Edna's arm. "Come upstairs, Miss Fisher. You've got to see this."

They all walked up the stairway to the front bedroom. Dan opened the door. There, on the floor, was a stub of a candle. Surrounding it was a pile of oil-soaked rags smoldering from a recently extinguished fire.

"If we hadn't come when we did, Miss Fisher, your place would have been ashes by morning," Dan said, quietly. "You, included, Edna."

Edna Fisher's knees wobbled. Her eyes rolled back and she collapsed at Kate's feet.

"That's it," Eddie said. He turned toward the stairway. "I'm going after Ronald right now."

"No!" Miss Fisher pleaded as she rose to her feet. "It can't be Ronald. It's someone else. I just know it. Please. I'll do anything. Don't hurt him."

Everyone hurried down the stairs to the front hall.

"You can't ignore this," Eddie said, standing next to the opened front door. "Look," he said to Miss Fisher, pointing to the dead squirrels. "Does this look like something a normal person would do?"

"Oh, my gracious," Edna exclaimed. She grabbed Pete's shoulder to steady herself.

"When we got here," Dan added, "someone was sneaking off your porch. We weren't sure who it was at the time, but it must have been Ronald. Who else could it be? The fire he set upstairs would have killed you. We have to call the police," he said, moving to the phone.

"No," Edna said. "Not the police. I don't care how much it looks like it was Ronald. He didn't do it. They'll take him away and lock him up forever. I owe it to my sister—to my father. We have to keep this a secret. Please, don't tell anyone. I must talk to Ronald."

"All right," Dan said, "Eddie and I will go after him."

"Please, be careful," she called out in tears. "Don't hurt him."

"Pete, Kate, stay with Miss Fisher," Dan said. "If we're not back in an hour, go tell Aunt and Uncle what's happening."

"He lives on French Lane behind the Lake View."

CHAPTER 16
"VOLUME ONE"

Dan and Eddie returned, their bikes coasting to a stop in front of Edna Fisher's cottage. "There was no sign of him anywhere," Eddie said to Pete, Kate, and Miss Fisher as they stood in the cool, night air.

"We even tried in town at the pool hall," Dan added.

"Do you know anything about an old book, Miss Fisher?" Dan asked as the five gathered in the front hall. "It might be a thick, blue one—maybe thirty or forty years old. Aunt Nancy says it has maps and stories about Mackinac Island."

"Sure," Edna Fisher said, looking surprised. "You must be talking about Ed Wood's book. He and my father were close friends—birds of a feather, you might say. Each loved this island and wrote about it constantly. Ed's book actually had two parts. Volume One had all the maps and actual history of Mackinac. Volume Two had the legends and stories of the people who visited here. My father helped Mr. Wood with it. It was published at about the same time as my father's book. The first, signed copy is in our library," Edna said. "You may look at that one, if you'd like."

"The copy in the library is missing," Eddie corrected. "There's a four-inch gap on the shelf where it belongs."

"I don't mean the public library," Miss Fisher replied. "I mean our own library. Mr. Wood's books were my father's most prized possession. He used to tell me, `This will be for you. It will be very valuable one day.' He told me that just before he died. He never explained what he meant. By then he was saying a lot of things like that."

"Can we see it?" Dan asked.

"Certainly, follow me." Edna Fisher led the way through a narrow door at the end of the hallway. She turned on a light and the five stood in a small, octagon-shaped room which was completely encircled by shelves of books.

"It's right here . . ." Miss Fisher began to reach over her head and then stopped. "It's missing," she gasped. "Volume Two is here, but the one with the maps is gone."

"Just our luck," Eddie said, shaking his head.

"I think it's more than luck," Dan said evenly. "Whoever's been messing up your house must also think that Volume One holds the key to the mystery."

"They have the book," Pete pointed out. "But they don't have the poem."

"I'm not so sure," Dan replied. "Remember? Two nights ago at the dinner table, Ronald was in the next room as we read it aloud. He may have heard the whole thing."

"Ronald could not have possibly memorized that poem," Edna Fisher defended. "He barely remembers his own name sometimes. It must be someone else."

"Maybe you're right, Miss Fisher," Kate said. "But someone is causing a lot of damage around here. If it's not Ronald, then who could it be?"

"What about those men in town he's been hanging around with?" Dan suggested. "Someone at the pool hall. Has Ronald said who he's been talking to?"

"Just one." Edna replied. "The owner, I believe his name is Pounders. Jim or Jack. No, Jake. Jake Pounders. But why would he do this to me?"

"Maybe he believes those old stories about your father stashing money away," Eddie said.

"If we can get Volume One and figure out the riddle in the poem," Kate said, "maybe we could beat him to the treasure. But I'll tell you what, I don't think whoever's behind all this will stop at anything to get what he wants."

"Including murder," Dan added, picking up the candle and the oil-soaked rags.

"Doesn't anyone else on this island have a copy of that book?" Pete asked.

"No," Edna shook her head. "It was the only . . . Wait. Emerson Dufina. Ed Wood thought the world of Emerson. So did my father. Emerson was a young man at the time, but Ed and my father took him under their wings like a son. All three of them studied Mackinac's history with a passion. They'd often sit on the green here at the Annex and talk about it for hours—attracted quite a crowd sometimes. If anyone else has a copy of *Historic Mackinac*, it's Emerson Dufina."

"Where does he live?" Dan asked anxiously.

"In the village," Edna replied. "On French Lane behind the Lake View."

"Could we call him?" Dan pursued.

"Sure. We'll do it tomorrow morning," Edna nodded.

"No, I mean, right now," Dan insisted.

"At this time of night?" Edna asked. "We couldn't do that."

"We need to know right now," Kate replied.

"He may not be there," Miss Fisher said. "He's a master carpenter and often works on the mainland."

"All the more reason," Dan said. "He may be off on the first boat in the morning."

Edna nodded. She went to the telephone stand and thumbed through a thin directory. She lifted the candlestick phone and dialed the number.

"Hello?" Edna said a moment later. "Emerson?"

"You may use the Straits Room to spread out your materials."

CHAPTER 17
THE KEY

At nine the next morning, the four teens stood at the doorstep of a small, frame house on French Street. A tall, grizzled old man in his seventies held the screen door and craned his neck looking out beyond his visitors.

"You can't be too sure," Mr. Dufina spoke in a hushed tone. "Especially with what Edna told me last night. You're welcome to come in and see the book, but I can't let it out of my sight. You understand."

"Sure," Dan nodded, leading the others into the darkened house. "It may be the only one left. Do you have the map and poem, Pete?"

"Right here," Pete said, following Kate inside. He slipped the leather carrying case from his back.

"Please, sit down," Emerson said. "I'll be right back."

The four friends pulled up chairs around the kitchen table as Mr. Dufina left the room. He came back a minute later with a thick, dark blue, book. Three gold crests of France, England, and the United States were on the front and the words, "Historic Mackinac, Edwin O. Wood." Underneath, it read, "Volume One."

"That's it," Kate whispered. She opened the front cover and turned to the table of contents. She glanced through the chapter titles. "Here it is," she said. "It's the last chapter, `Descriptive Notes on Names and Places at Mackinac Island—pages 507 to 606.'"

She turned to the back of the book. At page 507, she found a thin, three-part map folded into the binding. It was exactly like the one at the library, names and numbers included, except Miss Martin's hanging map was five times bigger than this one. Plus, the library one was outlined by brown-and-white scenes of Mackinac Island. But this one, the original map, had much more detail. Kate refolded it and turned to the next page. "Here's what we're looking for," she said. "Every name on the map has a number and something written about it."

"What we have to do now," Dan said, "is to look up all the places in the poem and mark them on our trail map. We've already checked the places that were named on the library map. Now we have to match the names of those places that are marked only by a number."

Pete opened his envelope and slid out the papers.

"Here we go, guys," Kate said. "What's the first pair, Pete," she asked anxiously.

"Illini Route and Fort Holmes Flag," Pete said, looking at the poem.

"We've got Fort Holmes Flag," Dan said. "We need to find what number Illini Route is." Dan thumbed through the book to the "I's. "Here it is," Dan said, "on page 548. It's number 34 on the map. It says it's named for the Illinois Indians, a tribe related to the Ojibways and Ottawas. Now, where's number 34 on the map?" Dan flipped the pages back to the map in the book and unfolded it.

"There it is," Eddie said, looking over Dan's shoulder. "Way up there by Griffin Cove."

"Mark that spot on the trail map, Pete," Dan said. "And put 'Illini Route' next to it, okay?"

"Got it," Pete said.

"How about the next one," Kate said, "Langlade Craig."

Dan flipped through to page 553. "Number 197," he said.

"Here it is, right above Hennepin Point," Dan said pointing to the southeast coast.

Pete carefully marked the spot on the bicycle map.

In fifteen minutes, the entire map was marked by the twenty locations in the poem.

"I don't get it," Pete said, leaning back and staring at the bicycle map. "Now we've got a whole bunch of dots all over the place. What does that prove?"

"I don't know either," Dan admitted. "I was hoping maybe they'd form an `X' or something."

"Well, if nothing else," Kate shrugged, "at least we can go to all of the places in the poem. Maybe when we get there we'll see something that ties them all together and leads us to the treasure."

"Mr. Dufina," Eddie said, "can you see anything that we're missing?"

"Nope," the elderly man said, shaking his head. "But if it's treasure you're looking for, you won't likely find anything any more valuable than what Lemuel put on paper. He had nothing of any great value except his love for this island. If any of that rubs off on you, well, that would be a treasure worth finding. If you do what Kate says and go to the places in his poem—and learn about each one of them—then that will be your treasure. Mackinac's history is so woven into world history that everything you learn will be a treasure of knowledge." Mr. Dufina arose from his chair and stood before his guests. He planted his gnarled fists firmly on the hardwood table. "You four have convinced me that you are serious in your efforts. I will loan this book to you for three days, but you must go to each of the places and read what the book says about them. If you don't, I'm coming after you, got it?" he said with a smile. "And you have to carry it safely. If anything happens to this book . . ." He leaned back from the table leaving his sentence unfinished. He then smiled at the four teenagers. "I'm sure that what you learn will be worth a hundred times what little wealth General Fisher may have stashed away."

"You really don't believe in the General's Treasure?" Kate asked.

"No," Emerson said. "Hundreds of people over the years have spent fortunes seeking it. All have left empty-handed. But if you want to look, the book is yours under those conditions."

"We'll do it," Kate said. "It will fit perfectly in my uncle's Civil War bag."

"And we promise to read about each place," Dan said.

"What's the first one, Dan?" Eddie asked, getting up from his chair.

Dan looked at the map. "Haldimand Bay," he said. "Let's go, guys. We'll be careful with your book, Mr. Dufina."

The four marched out of the French Lane house into the sunlight of a cool, clean, Mackinac Island morning. The crowds had not yet filled the streets when they hopped on their bikes and headed for the harbor.

———

"Here we are," Eddie said, slowing his bike. "'Haldimand Bay,' it's called in the book. People now just call it 'the harbor.' There's not much to see here."

"Unless you're seeing it for the first time," Dan disagreed.

89

"I think that's the point," Kate said. "We've always taken this place for granted, haven't we? Coming here from the Snows and docking at the marina became routine for us. But remember the first time we came, Dan?"

"I'll say," Dan said. "We were five years old. It was a day trip where a whole bunch of Les Cheneaux people came here in their power boats. It was a dead-calm morning. Kate and I played on the deck of the *Polly Ann* as we crossed Lake Huron. When we came into the harbor my dad picked me up on his shoulders and said, `This is Mackinac Island.' He turned from side to side. `This is the most historic island in all America.' I didn't know what he meant, but I'll never forget what I saw. It was awesome."

Kate reached for Mr. Dufina's book. "Let's see what it says."

She opened the leather bag and turned to the back looking up the entry under "Haldimand Bay."

She read aloud, "`General Sir Frederick Haldimand was the British Governor of Canada during the American Revolution. He served in the French and Indian War. Haldimand Bay is the first place on Mackinac Island to be named for a British citizen.'"

"Where to now, Dan?" Eddie asked.

They continued for the next two hours stopping and reading about each of the places named in the General's poem.

———

"The last one," Dan said, checking off Tom Scott's Cave, "is Fort Holmes Flag. It's just up the road."

"Well, we're almost there," Eddie said, leading the pack.

"Hey, look," Kate yelled. "Someone's running off into the woods?"

MACKINAC ISLAND
MICHIGAN

Point Aux Pins

Pontiac's Lookout

Agatha Outlook

LAKE HURON

Point Holmes

Fort Holmes

Fort Alexander Hamilton

Deer Park

Public Pasture

Haldimand Bay

Biddle's Pt.

Julia Pt.

Tonti Spring
Hennepin Pt.
Languade Craig
Sentinel Rock
Baby Manitou
Wigley Waterspout
Arch Rock
Gitchie Manitou
Michabous Landing
Menard Station
Allouez Cascade
Dwightwood Spring
Manitou
Echo Grotto
Fairy Kitchen
Parkman Prospect
Fairy Arch
Giant's Stairway
Family Rocks
Robinson's Folly
Presque Beach
Ferry Beach
Mission Pt.

Skull Cave
Lime Kiln
Sugar Loaf
Old Quarry
Arch Rock
Rifle Range
Garrison Trail
Rock Trail
Winnebago
Huron Road
Manitou Trail

Wishing Spring
Old Distillery Road
Cadotte Ave.
White Beach

"He's got a shovel," Dan said, pumping for all he was worth.

"I'm going after him," Pete said.

"Eddie, go with Pete," Dan said. "Kate, follow me. We'll see what he was digging for."

The four split up, Pete and Eddie dropping their bikes and Dan and Kate riding along the dirt road to the fort.

"There he is," Eddie yelled. "He's right on the edge of the Turtle's Back. Hurry, Pete!"

Pete made his last pump to get off his bike and caught his right pant leg in the sprocket. By the time he'd gotten it loose, Eddie was almost out of sight in the forest. Pete raced to catch up and finally found him standing in a clearing.

"Lost him," Eddie said.

"Sorry," Pete groaned.

"Not your fault," Eddie said. "I can't figure it. He wasn't twenty feet in front of me when I looked down to jump over a rock. When I looked up, he was gone."

"He's got to be around here somewhere," Pete said. "Are there any caves or anything like that?"

"They're everywhere," Eddie replied. "This island has more holes and hiding places than a Harry Houdini hat. We could be standing on top of him and we wouldn't know it."

Pete looked at his feet. There were fresh footprints leading to a rock formation which dropped down a cliff to a road below. "Well, he's gone now," Pete muttered.

Dan and Kate circled around the west side of the Fort Holmes rampart to the south gate. There at the flag pole four holes had been made in the ground.

"I'll bet it was Ronald," Kate said. "Let's go tell Miss Fisher."

"Wait a minute," Dan said, hopping off his bike. "I want to see what he was digging into. Maybe we can tell if he found anything before he took off into the woods."

Dan knelt by the flag pole. "What do you see?" Kate asked anxiously.

"I'm not sure," Dan whispered. "It looks as if he might have gotten a can or something out of the bottom of this hole."

Kate glanced up as Eddie and Pete approached on their bikes. "Who was it?" Kate called out.

"Couldn't tell for sure," Eddie said, setting his kickstand. "He just vanished right before my eyes."

"I think the guy was on a treasure hunt," Dan said. "And he may have found what he was looking for."

"It's getting dark," Eddie said. "Let's get back to your aunt and uncle's."

"Not yet," Kate said. "We promised Mr. Dufina we'd read about each place."

"Okay," Eddie said, looking at his watch. "But make it snappy. It's too early to be this dark. I don't like the looks of those clouds over there."

"All right," Kate said, turning the pages in the old book. "'Fort Holmes: Built by the British soon after the capture of Mackinac in 1812. The British . . .'"

"That's enough," Eddie interrupted. "Let's go. We'll read the rest later. I just saw a bolt of lightening."

Kate put the book in the leather pouch and the four tore off on their bikes toward the west bluff. There was still plenty of daylight as they approached the Grand Hotel golf course, but the sky had taken on an odd, yellowish cast. A black cloud bank filled the northwestern sky, and a cold wind smacked the four bikers in the face as they came over the rise.

CHAPTER 18
RESEARCH

They hadn't gotten a hundred yards farther ahead when the black skies opened. Forty mile-an-hour winds and sheets of rain ripped into the four bikers' faces.

"Come on," Dan yelled, leading the pack. "The barn's just ahead!"

BB-sized hail pellets stung their faces as they raced single-file along the narrow road. Dan peeked occasionally over his handlebars to keep from driving off into the woods. The others followed close behind, each keeping their eyes only on the rear wheel of the rider in front of them.

"Sharp right!" Dan yelled as he turned into the barn. Kate, Eddie, and Pete flew through the doorway. Larger hunks of hail began to blast the roof magnifying the clamor of the thunderstorm.

"That was close," Kate shivered. "I'll bet the temperature's dropped thirty degrees in ten minutes."

"All we have to do now is to run across the path to the back door," Eddie said. "I say we head for it now."

"The storm might blow over in a few minutes," Pete said.

"Maybe," Eddie said. "Or it could go on all night."

"Okay," Dan said, peeking around the slit in the door. "Let's make a run for it. Ready?"

Everyone nodded.

"Go!" Dan yelled. He pushed the barn door a foot to the right and shot across the path. The other three followed and the four practically fell into the kitchen. They got to their feet and brushed the rain from their clothes.

Kate opened the leather pouch. "At least Mr. Dufina's book didn't get wet," Kate said.

"You had me worried," Nancy Anderson said, coming from the living room. "I was afraid you might miss dinner. We're having a special treat tonight. I hope you'll like it."

_____

Pete hadn't been seated at the dining table more than ten seconds before Chef Zachary plopped a huge, red crablike thing on his plate.

"Holy mackerel," Pete whispered to Eddie. "Where do you find crayfish this big?"

"That's not a crayfish," Eddie whispered back. "It's a lobster."

Pete tapped the red shell with his knife. "How do you eat it?" Pete asked.

"Well, it isn't easy, but it's worth it. Just watch me," Eddie said as he picked up a nutcracker.

"How was your day, kids?" Nancy Anderson asked.

"Fine," Dan answered. "Up until the storm hit. Any idea how long this weather's going to last, Uncle George?"

"The radio says it should break during the night," Mr. Anderson replied. "What have you four been up to?"

"We've just been checking out the places in the poem that Pete got from Edna Fisher," Dan said.

"We found a copy of that blue history book you told us about, Aunt Nancy," Kate added. "Emerson Dufina, a friend of Edna Fisher, lent it to us. He told us he'd let us use it if we read about each of the places in the poem."

"This could be the best night of the summer for that," Nancy Anderson said. "Why don't you spread out your things in the Straits Room?"

"Good idea," Kate said. "We'll read about the places in the poem for tomorrow."

"Is everyone done with their dessert?" Dan asked.

Kate, Eddie, and Pete nodded.

"May we be excused, Uncle George?" Dan asked. "We'd like to get started."

"You may," George Anderson said. "We'll be going to the Music Room at the Grand for the evening, but we won't be late."

Kate got up from the table and the three boys followed her to the circular room overlooking the Straits. The rain and wind pelted the large, stained glass windows, but the horizon to the west was a bright, saffron yellow, a good sign for the next day's weather. The four spread out the book, poem, and map in front of them on the round table.

"I still think General Fisher buried something," Dan said, "and the key to finding it is in this poem."

"It sure is strange," Kate said, "that exactly half of the places in the poem are written on the map, and the rest are only numbered."

For the next three hours they plotted lines and read the passages from the book describing life over the last three centuries in Mackinac Country. They had just finished reading about Father Marquette when Eddie spoke up.

"I've never thought about how dangerous life was back then," he said. "Those missionaries, guys like Marquette,

Dablon, and Charlevoix, really stuck their necks out just coming here. And if they stumbled into some angry Indians, their sermons might not last very long."

"Yeah, about as long as their hair cuts," Pete said, making a chopping motion across the top of his head.

"And the explorers," Eddie said, "Champlain, Joliet, and LaSalle—what wild times they must have had—cold winters, bug-infested summers, rain, wind . . ."

"How about the fur traders," Dan added, "going into the woods for nine or ten months with nothing but what they could carry on their backs? I'll never understand how they did that."

"That couldn't have been any cakewalk," Eddie said, "but can you picture canoeing around the Great Lakes like they all did? These stories make it sound as if they were always going from Montreal to Green Bay or Detroit and then up and down the Mississippi—like we go into town for a loaf of bread or something—and in birch bark canoes, no less."

"Look, I don't know what's keeping you three going," Pete yawned, "but I'm bushed. I'm going up to bed. See you in the morning. Sweet dreams," he smiled at Kate. "And for you and Dan, I really mean it. No more three a.m. bike rides, okay?"

That bike wasn't there this afternoon, Pete thought.

CHAPTER 19
LIGHT IN THE NIGHT

Pete awakened with a start. The bedroom was cool, but he was sweating bullets. He'd been having a nightmare that he knew was a dream but was so real that every time he woke up, he couldn't get it out of his head. He'd fall back asleep and dream it all over again. In it he was carrying the poem, and he was being stalked. Everywhere he looked, a man was just ducking out of sight. He opened his eyes but the room was pitch black. He didn't want to go back to sleep because he knew the dream would continue and this time the guy would get the poem. It was dumb, he knew that, but he couldn't help himself. He had to get up. *Maybe if I walk around for awhile I could dream about something else—Kate, maybe. Why couldn't I dream about Kate? I wouldn't mind that.*

Pete slid out of bed and worked his way over to the window. He pulled aside the curtain and looked three stories down onto the path in front of the Anderson cottage. The moon was high and cast short shadows. His eyes were drawn to the wooden fence along the west bluff. A bike, almost covered in shadows, was leaning up against

97

it. *That wasn't there this afternoon*, he thought. *We would have seen it while we were working on the map. So where did it come from?* He immediately thought of Ronald Sawyer, Edna Fisher's nephew. *What if he's spying on us right now, looking in the windows? Or what if he's inside trying to find the poem? What did Edna say—that once Ronald wanted something, he'd do anything to get it? Where had they left it?* Pete was sure it was still on the table in the Straits Room. He heard a creak outside his door. Someone was in the hallway. Pete froze. Any second and the door would fly open and the menacing beady eyes of the stubby little man would be staring Pete in the face.

Pete dropped to his knees. He scrunched on his belly and slid under the bed. He lay there breathing as quietly as he could.

Whoever was outside his door had heard Pete move. *He's waiting*, Pete thought. *He wants me to make the first move. Well, I'm not going to.*

Five minutes passed. The only sound was the pounding of Pete's heart growing louder by the minute. He inched his way to the door. He reached up to the doorknob, put his hand on it, and turned it slightly. It creaked and Pete fully expected it to fly open with the hideous man standing over him. But nothing happened. He turned the knob further. The light in the hallway pierced the tiny crack in the doorway. He put his eye as near to the opening as he could and pulled on the handle. No one was there. Pete got to his feet and poked his head into the hall. All the bedroom doors were closed. He worked his way to the stairway.

He moved silently down to the second floor—then to the living room. A light was on in the Straits Room. Was Ronald there right now? Pete glanced around the corner and saw the top of someone's head in the circular room.

Someone is sitting exactly where I was not two hours ago. It must be Ronald. His mind spun in horror. He had to get closer to make sure it was Edna's nephew, but he knew what might happen if he got caught. The small, muscular man would grab him and snap his neck. Pete knelt on the floor and crawled past a wicker rocking chair. He tried to peek out from behind the sofa. A book shelf blocked his view. He reached with his right hand to move ahead. He bumped his shoulder against the leg of an end table and a heavy, stone figurine thudded hard on the floor.

The person in the Straits Room jumped from his chair.

Pete recoiled behind the sofa.

"Who's there?" came a voice. A light switch clicked on and footsteps ran toward him.

Pete looked up. Standing next to him with an andiron poised over his head was Dan.

"Pete!" Dan whispered. "What in the world are you doing?"

"Breathing, still," Pete sighed. "No thanks to you. What are you doing out there? You should wear a sign on your head or something. You nearly scared me to death."

"Come here," Dan said, picking up the stone statue. "I couldn't get to sleep so I came back down here. Something you said this afternoon kept bugging me. Remember when you told us that maybe we couldn't see the bait for all the worms? Well, it got me to thinking. I've diagramed each pair of places in the poem every way I could think of. So far, nothing seems to work, but I'm just sure the answer is in here somewhere."

Pete slowly got to his feet and followed Dan into the Straits Room. There was the map with a pencil and ruler. Lines were everywhere.

"I had almost given up when you came, Pete," Dan said. "Let's do this: We're just going to stare at this thing for five minutes. Then we'll see what we've come up with. Okay?"

Pete nodded and took a seat at the table. A pencil and pad of paper lay nearby. Pete jotted down the first letter of each place, "I-F-M-L, H-G-H-S, O-F-T-D, W-B-C-S, C-T-B-N." *Boy, if there's a clue in there, it's hidden pretty good*, he thought. He tried the second letters. Nothing. He lined up some of the points with the ruler. First to second. Third to forth. They didn't cross.

"I give up, Dan," Pete said. "I'm tired. What time is it."

"Midnight," Dan said. "I'm going to bed, too. See you in the morning."

"I'm taking the paper and Mr. Dufina's book upstairs to my bedroom," Pete said. "I'd never get back to sleep now if I don't put them somewhere safe."

"I've got just the place for them," Dan said. "There's a secret room on the third floor by our bedrooms."

"You're kidding," Pete exclaimed. "A secret room? Where?"

"You'd never find it," Dan smiled. "Aunt and Uncle use it to store their silverware and other stuff in the winter. Come on."

"Maybe now I can sleep without any more stalking dreams," Pete said. "I was having the worst nightmare. Someone was chasing me all over the place trying to get the poem. When I woke up I looked outside and saw a bike against the fence. That's why I came down here. All I could think about was that it might belong to whoever was in my dream—spying on us and looking for the poem."

"This whole thing is making you crazy, Pete," Dan smiled.

"Yeah, that was the worst dream ever."

"Well, let's get upstairs," Dan said, glancing around the room. "Maybe we should take a minute and clean up. I wouldn't want Aunt Nancy to get mad at us for leaving a mess. You get the popcorn bowls and glasses and I'll wipe the table, okay?"

"All right," Pete said, reaching for a glass. Something outside caught his eye. "Dan, look!" Pete yelled. He pointed to the fence along the West Bluff Road. "Someone's taking the bike."

"What? Where?" Dan said, rushing to the window.

"Did you see him?" Pete gasped.

"See who?"

"The guy that took the bike I was telling you about," Pete said.

"Holy cow," Dan whispered. "Do you think it was Ronald?"

"Who else?" Pete said.

"I don't know about you, Pete," Dan said, "but I have the oddest feeling that someone's watching everything we do. Whoever it is must think we have something that's worth a lot."

"The only thing we have now that we didn't have before is that book," Pete said.

"But if it's Ronald, he's already got Edna's book. No, I think he's still after the poem. That's even more reason to make me think the answer is right in front of us," Dan said holding the poem and the book.

Pete's heart was still racing after seeing the bike being whisked right from under his nose.

The two went upstairs, Pete carrying the book, poem and map. Dan walked past his room but not quite to Pete's. He stopped at a narrow door in the hallway, turned, and smiled at Pete.

"Linen closet, right?" he said opening the door.

Pete looked in and saw shelves of sheets, blankets, and towels. "Yeah? What of it?"

"Presto," Dan said. He flicked a lever above the door and the whole cabinet rolled back into a dark room. He hit a button and a light went on inside revealing a ten-foot by ten-foot chamber. Shelves and drawers lined the windowless walls. A globe, four feet in diameter, sat on a wooden stand in the middle of the room. Dan walked over to it, twisted the northern hemisphere fifteen degrees to the west, and pressed a spot in the southwestern part of England. A whirling of small gears began, and slowly the entire continent of Africa separated itself from its surrounding oceans. A large, velvet-lined box opened up in the very core of the earth.

Pete's jaw fell to his chest. He stood awe-stricken holding the book, poem, and map. Dan set them inside and punched a spot near Cairo, Egypt. Africa rolled back into place.

"How's this for secure?" Dan said, turning the northern hemisphere back to the east.

"Well, if this is the best you can do . . ." Pete said, a slow grin crossing his face.

"I hope you don't have any more nightmares," Dan smiled.

The two turned from the globe and went back into the hall. Dan hit the light switch and flipped another lever. The linen closet shelves rolled back into place, and Dan closed the door.

"Good night," Dan said.

"G`night," Pete said, still shaking his head.

*"Great news! We've been invited aboard the **South American**."*

CHAPTER 20
DAY 6 THE *SOUTH AMERICAN*

"Good morning," Mrs. Anderson said as her four guests trailed down the stairs to the living room. "Great news. We have been invited aboard the *South American*. Mr. Hewlett, the *South*'s captain, and Mr. Lang, the owner of the Arnold Transit Company, are treating us to brunch."

"No kidding?" Dan exclaimed. "What time will she be docking?"

"Ten o'clock," Nancy Anderson replied.

"Great. We'll be able to see the whole thing," Eddie said. "This is the best, Pete."

"What's the *South American*?" Pete asked.

"Only the largest cruise ship in the Great Lakes," Kate said. "She's five hundred feet long and ten stories high. You'll be able to see her all the way from Bois Blanc."

"And when her whistle blows," Dan added, "you'll have to hold on to something just to stay on the dock. The passengers will be lined up along the railings and the crew will be scurrying around like crazy."

"Charles is rigging the black landau and will meet us at the front gate in half an hour," Nancy advised. "Run upstairs and put on your best clothes."

———

The *South American* swept majestically into Mackinac harbor. Mr. and Mrs. Anderson and their guests stood at the head of the pier as the immense cruise ship approached the dock. From the top of the nearest smokestack, Pete saw a huge billow of white steam shoot into the air. Almost immediately, a crushing, low-pitched whistle shook him. It thundered on for what seemed like forever vibrating his whole body at a pitch so low it was almost inaudible. Still, it came with such force that he clamped his hands to his ears and turned his head. He glanced at Kate. She had her ears covered, too, but was smiling as though this was just about the most wonderful thing that had ever happened. Eddie, Dan—everyone was doing the same as Kate. What could possibly be so terrific about having your brains blown out by a steam whistle? Would it ever stop? Wasn't the idea to let the people on the dock know that the boat would be landing? Pete couldn't imagine anyone in the entire Upper Peninsula not knowing it.

Kate nudged Pete. "What's holding you up? Come on."

Pete blinked. The rest of the party was thirty yards ahead moving toward the gangplank. "Um, sorry, I guess I was thinking about something else." Kate took Pete's hand and the two hurried to catch up to the others.

In minutes the ship was tied to the dock and the passengers were filing past Pete toward town. Pete and the other guests were greeted by Captain Hewlett and Mr. Lang who walked with them to the bridge.

"You four can look around here for a while," the captain said. "I'll show the adults to the dining salon."

104

Dan picked up the captain's binoculars and scanned the village. "There's Market Street," he said, focussing the glasses over the top of the Main Street buildings. "And there's the library," he continued. "I could find a freckle on a frog with these babies."

"Let me try them," Eddie said.

Dan handed the field glasses to Eddie.

"There's Miss Martin going to the library," Eddie said. "She must be late today. She's just opening up."

"Someone's going in right after her," Kate said, squinting without the aid of the binoculars. "Eddie, did you see who that was?"

"No," Eddie said, fidgeting with the adjustment screw.

"Whoever it is, closed the door in a hurry," Kate said. "Did you get a look at him, Dan?" she asked, glancing warily at her brother.

"It looked like Ronald Sawyer," Dan breathed.

"That's what I thought, too," Kate said. "We've got to get there fast. Miss Martin might be in trouble."

"But we can't leave now," Pete said. "Lunch will be in a few minutes."

"You're right, Pete," Dan said. "Eddie, I'll tell Aunt and Uncle that you had to run into town. Kate, you stay here with Pete and watch for Eddie. Eddie, if nothing's wrong, just come back. But if there is, wave your arms. Kate will be watching with the binoculars, and we'll come running. Got it?"

"Got it," Eddie nodded and spun away from the bridge.

Two minutes later Eddie had reached the gangplank and was walking quickly along the pier to the head of the dock. Kate and Pete watched as Eddie worked his way through the crowd and up to the library. He stopped at the door and turned to be sure that Kate and Pete were still watching. Kate waved, and Eddie went in.

A minute passed. Finally, the door opened and Eddie stepped out putting his hands in front of him as if to say, "I don't get it," and then began to walk back toward the harbor.

Kate and Pete waved and turned from the bridge.

———

It was a wonderful lunch. Shrimp cocktails and vichyssoise were followed by hearts of palm salad, Lobster Thermidor, chocolate eclairs, and finally, iced tea and macadamia nuts.

It wasn't until the four were alone walking toward the Anderson's carriage at the head of the dock that Eddie was able to tell what had happened at the library.

"I don't understand," Eddie said. "Miss Martin told me that Ronald Sawyer didn't come in.

"You must be joking," Dan responded.

"Nope," Eddie shook his head.

"I was sure that it was Ronald," Kate said. "If not, it was his double."

"I didn't think anyone could look like Ronald Sawyer," Dan said with a smile.

"Well, you saw me go in, Kate," Eddie said, "but no one was around. I checked all three aisles, even went to the end of them. No one was there. Then I went to the back where Miss Martin has her office. She said that someone had wanted directions to Jack's Livery, but other than that, no one had come by."

"Let's forget it," Dan said. "The rest of the afternoon is ours. Maybe we should do something besides worry about Edna Fisher's problems."

"Right," Kate agreed. "It's getting hot. I say we go to the Grand for a swim. Maybe this heat is making us see things."

At the head of the dock they joined Mr. and Mrs. Anderson and boarded the black carriage.

"Let's go for a swim."

CHAPTER 21
A FURTHER CLUE

"I can't help but think about Miss Fisher," Kate said as the four stepped from the carriage. "We've been to every place on the map, studied Mr. Dufina's book, practically memorized the poem, and we're still no closer than when we started."

"Maybe there is no pot of gold," Eddie sighed. "Maybe Mr. Dufina was right and General Fisher didn't bury anything."

"No," Dan said. "There is something. I can feel it. It's staring us in the face. We've just got to put the clues together. Let's get changed and go for a swim. Maybe something will come up. At least, it'll cool us off," he smiled.

"Where's Pete?" Kate asked as the other two boys came down the stairs to the living room. There they stood, Dan, Kate, and Eddie wearing, over their swimsuits, a complete outfit of swim wear—deck shoes, tank top, terry cloth robe, and sun hat—each matching perfectly. They looked more like they were going to a formal party than for a swim.

"I don't know," Eddie said. "Let's hope he hasn't gone into another one of his mind muddles."

Just then Pete came down the stairs. He was wearing his old swimming trunks, a tattered tee-shirt, and his floppy basketball shoes. He glanced at the others who stared at him as if he had already committed a federal offence.

"We'll have to borrow some of Uncle George's stuff," Kate said to Dan. "They won't even let us on the grounds unless we're all in proper dress."

"We'll be back in a jiff," Dan said. "Come on, Pete."

The two ran up one flight of stairs to Uncle George's bedroom. Dan knocked. Nobody answered, so he went in. In seconds he came out with a tank top, robe, deck slippers, and hat."

"Here you go, Pete," Dan said. "This will get us in."

"Aren't we forgetting something?" Pete said.

"I don't think so," Dan thought. "Shoes, shirt, jacket and hat. Nope, it's all there. Come on."

"No, I mean, check this out," Pete smiled, putting on Uncle George's robe. It draped over his shoulders and dragged on the floor. He slipped George Anderson's size thirteen deck slippers right over his own basketball shoes. They looked like water skis. He popped the hat on his head and it dropped over his ears. "Before I only looked like a bum. Now, if you could just find me a big, red nose and some white greasepaint, I could go as Clarabelle the Clown," he laughed.

"Hmm," Dan smiled, "I get the point. Okay, I've got it. Bring the stuff downstairs."

In minutes, the four were hurrying along the Grand Hotel porch. Eddie was wearing Uncle George's pool clothes and Pete had on Eddie's. Now, the two of them both looked like clowns, but not so much that they couldn't get past the Grand Hotel's fashion patrol. They quickly

108

made their way along the path to the pool. Dan showed his pass to the attendant and the four were each given a towel. They stepped around the edge of the long, kidney-shaped pool past rows of deck chairs. People of all ages were stretched out sunbathing. Pete noticed a four-year-old boy shaking uncontrollably next to his mother who was rubbing him vigorously with two fluffy towels.

"Here we are," Kate said as she removed her beach robe and stood at the far end of the pool.

There was not one ripple on the surface, and the water was crystal clear. Eddie and Dan were soon standing next to her as Pete glanced around at the other guests. A few had set down their magazines and books to watch the four newcomers get ready to dive into the deep end.

Kate bent over, swung her arms back, and then shot forward. She stretched out in a perfect racing dive and was followed immediately by Dan and Eddie. They stroked their way toward the shallow end.

Nobody said anything about a race, Pete thought as he deposited his shoes, shirt, and jacket on a nearby chaise. *I'm a pretty fast swimmer. I bet I could beat at least one of them.* He hurried up to the edge and noticed that now everybody was watching the three swimmers—the ONLY swimmers in the entire pool. *That's odd, no one else seems to want to swim. I wonder what everybody's grinning about?* In the next instant he dived headlong into the clear water. Not only was the water clear, but immediately, everything else became clear, as well—why his friends were swimming so fast—why everyone was watching them—why so many people were grinning—why the little boy was being rubbed so hard. It was simple. Someone had filled the pool with ice water.

"Yeow!" Pete screamed, his head breaking the surface. He did an abrupt about-face and practically levitated out of the pool. He dashed for the deck chair and grabbed Eddie's terry cloth robe—the big one belonging to Uncle George—and wrapped himself in it.

His teeth were chattering as he watched Kate do a flip turn at the other end and start back toward him. Dan and Eddie were right behind gaining on her with every stroke, but Kate touched the end ahead of them. She bounded out of the water grinning like she'd just won an Olympic gold medal.

"Well, Pete," she said, reaching casually for her towel, "are you going to get in. The water's great."

"I've already been, thank you," he shivered. "I think I'll just grab a few rays."

Dan and Eddie followed Kate and immediately began toweling off.

"Bracing," Dan said, drawing a deep breath and smiling to Pete. "Aren't you going in?"

"No. And don't be `bracing' me. You know I hate cold water. You tricked me."

"What do you mean," Dan laughed.

"You know what I mean," Pete shuttered. "`Bracing,' my foot. I'll get you for this."

———

Pete slowly thawed and stretched out on the chaise. Soon the sun had dried him and he was actually becoming uncomfortably warm, not something he would have predicted a few minutes before.

"We'd better get back to Aunt and Uncle's. Dinner will be ready pretty soon," Kate said.

"Don't look now," Pete said, nodding toward a tree on the Grand Hotel lawn. "But I think that's Ronald Sawyer over there behind that pine."

"It sure is," Dan replied, glancing out of the corner of his eye. "I wonder what he's doing here. You don't suppose he's spying on us, do you?"

"Let's see if we can't sneak up on him," Kate said. "I'd like to hear what he says."

The four dressed and turned their towels in at the swim house, but when they looked for Ronald under the tree, he was gone.

"He's either a lot smarter than he let's on," Eddie said, "or we're not as clever as we think we are. That's the third time he's given us the slip."

"Well, we can't be chasing after him now," Kate said. "We'll be late for dinner."

"Uncle George and I will be at the Yacht Club."

CHAPTER 22
MIDSUMMER'S MORNING

"Thanks for the great dinner, Aunt Nancy," Dan said as he slid his chair from the table. "And thanks for taking us aboard the *South American* for lunch, Uncle George."

"It was our pleasure," Mr. Anderson said.

"If it's all right," Kate said, "we'd like to go into the Straits Room for a while. We've got some more stuff to work on."

"That would be fine, Kate," Nancy Anderson said. "George and I will be at the yacht club for the evening. You four may plan tomorrow's activities down here."

———

"Let's lay the map out again, Pete," Dan said pulling up his chair in the round room overlooking the bluff. "Bring the book, okay?"

The four friends filed into their study area off the Anderson's living room. Dan spread out the bicycle maps, and Pete set General Fisher's poem next to Mr. Dufina's book.

"Okay," Dan said, "we've got everything that General Fisher left for his daughters to find his treasure." Dan stood back and stared at his friends. "This whole poem was supposed to tell them how to find the money he stashed. But he never got the message to them. It could be that he was trying to keep it a secret from Alexa's husband. Now, with Alexa gone, the entire treasure belongs to Edna Fisher. Unless we hurry though, someone else will get it. I'll bet he's trying to solve the same riddle we are right now."

"What makes you so sure?" Eddie asked.

"Too many things have happened," Dan whispered. "Someone's watching us everywhere we go. Seeing Ronald at the pool was the final straw. He may not be clever enough to be at the bottom of this, but if not, then someone else is telling him what to do."

———

"It's getting late," Kate said. "Let's start tomorrow morning on a fresh track."

"Okay," Dan said. "Pete and I will put the stuff away."

"Right," Pete said. "Sweet dreams, everyone."

All four trudged upstairs. Dan and Pete slipped into the secret room, set their things in the globe safe, and then headed for their beds.

Pete went into a deep sleep, but at about two in the morning, he bolted up in his bed. He was having a dream. Chief Manabozho stood before him and then walked into his tepee. Then Pete gave a little jump and began to soar all over the Island. Pete normally loved flying dreams, but this one became so weird that it was getting more like a nightmare than a fantasy. In it, he skimmed over the tops of trees going from one point on Mackinac Island to another. He woke up after every trip but then continued the same dream going on to new places, starting or ending at all of the sites in General Fisher's poem. The weirdest thing, though, was that no matter where he started and landed, he always flew over Fort Holmes.

Pete got up with the first light of dawn. He dressed quickly, went to the secret room, and carried the map, book, and poem downstairs. He spread them on the Straits Room table and picked up the pencil. By now there were lines all over the map where they had tried to sketch out a solution to the poem's clues. Pete pulled out a fresh bike map and set to work. He remembered how Fort Holmes was in every one of his dreams, so he set his pencil right over it. He took the ruler and started with the last verse of the poem.

He made a line connecting the first and second sites, Charlevoix Heights and Turtle Back, but it didn't come close to Fort Holmes. Neither did the first and third. But the first and fourth, Charlevoix Heights and the North-east Crack, came pretty close. He drew a line connecting them. Then he checked the second and third points. The line from Baraga View to Turtle Back crossed right over Fort Holmes!

Holy cow! Pete thought. *I might be on to something.* He glanced back at the poem to the next-to-the-last verse. *Where are the next four places? One to four, 'Wawashkamo Links to Schoolcraft Rest,' that's pretty close.* He drew the line. *Two to three, 'Carver Pond to Breakwater West.' Man, oh man! Another 'X' so close to Fort Holmes that it can't just be blind luck.*

Just then Dan, Kate, and Eddie came down the stairs and saw Pete with his head bent over the map. "You're up early, Pete," Dan yawned.

At the sound of Dan's voice Pete jerked his head and just about jumped out of his chair. He turned and the three stepped back astonished by the shock in Pete's eyes. His face was ashen, almost transparent as though he'd seen a ghost.

"What's the matter, Pete?" Dan asked. "You're not still mad at me about the swimming pool thing, are you?"

"No," Pete replied seriously, "I might have just stumbled onto a clue here. Maybe there is something to the Indians' belief in dreams. Last night I had a real doozy. First, I dreamed about an Indian named Chief Manabozho. He was standing on the shore and waved for me to follow him as he walked toward his tepee. Then he disappeared inside, and I began to fly from one place to another all over the Island. The odd thing is is that no matter where I took off and landed, I always flew over Fort Holmes. I think the dream was trying to tell me that Fort Holmes is the key to the poem." Pete turned and faced the map. "So, when I woke up, I came down here. What I did was to start out with the answer and try to make the right question. Here, take a look at this." Pete pointed to the two X's.

"Right over Fort Holmes," Dan breathed. "What about the rest of the verses?"

"I've done the last two. I was about to do the next one," Pete said. "Here, Dan, you draw the lines." Pete's hand was shaking as he gave the ruler and pencil to Dan. "The third verse goes like this:

'Old Fort Garden, Forest King,
Tom Scott's Cave, Dwightwood Spring.'

So, you draw a line from the first one, Old Fort Garden, to the fourth, Dwightwood Spring. That's right. Now, from the second, Forest King, to the third, Scott's Cave."

"That is weird," Eddie whispered. "It's too close to Fort Holmes to be pure luck."

"You know what this means, don't you?" Dan said slumping into a chair. "It means we're too late."

"Too late for what?" Pete asked.

"Fort Holmes is where we saw that guy running into the woods the other day, remember?" Dan explained.

"Four fresh holes were dug into ground around the flag pole. I think we must have gotten there just as he was running off with the treasure."

"If that's so," Kate argued, "then why all the other stuff that's been going on around here since then."

"I don't know," Dan said, shaking his head. "Maybe he's worried that we'll figure out who he is and make him give the treasure to Edna Fisher."

"Let's see where the other places line up," Eddie interrupted. "Read the next verse, Pete."

"Okay," Pete said, looking down at the poem. "It starts with Haldimand Bay and ends with Sinclair Grove."

They watched as Dan made a line.

"Then it's Hennepin Point to Griffin Cove," Pete continued.

"This is so strange," Dan said. "The lines cross almost at Fort Holmes, but not quite, even if I cheat a little on the beginning and ending points. Let's do the last verse and see what happens there."

"Okay," Pete said. "Illini Route to Langlade Craig and Marquette Park to Fort Holmes Flag. What does that do?"

"Same thing," Dan said. "Close, but no kewpie."

"Maybe the General wasn't very good with straight lines," Eddie guessed.

"I don't think that's it," Kate argued. "Didn't Edna say that her father was a surveyor early in his army career?"

"You don't suppose," Pete wondered aloud, "that the bicycle trail map that we've been using could be off somehow? Or that when I put the numbers from the book onto the map that I didn't put them exactly in the right place?"

"Maybe that's it, Pete," Dan breathed. "Let's use the original map in Mr. Dufina's book."

"We don't dare write on that," Kate said. "He'd kill us."

"No, but we could copy it," Dan suggested.

"I've got some tracing paper in my room," Kate said. "I'll get it."

Kate bounded up the stairs and returned in seconds.

Dan opened the book to page 507 and unfolded the map. Kate placed the thin paper over it and began tracing. In twenty minutes she had a perfect replica of the *Historic Mackinac* map.

"Okay, Pete," Dan said. "Let's start all over. Read the first verse." Pete did and Dan drew the lines. "There must be a mistake," Dan said. "The intersection isn't at Fort Holmes at all. It crosses near there but it lines up perfectly with Sugar Loaf Rock. Let's try the next verse."

Seconds later, Dan had drawn another "X" on the new map. Dan stared amazed.

"Look at that," Eddie said. "It intersects right over the other one. Do the next verse, Dan."

Pete read the third verse, and the fourth and fifth. Each crossed precisely at Sugar Loaf Rock.

Dan leaned back in his chair and looked up at his friends. "The message from your dream wasn't about Fort Holmes, Pete," he said slowly. "It was that Chief Manabozho wanted you to come to his tepee. I think we need to go for a bike ride."

"I don't get it," Pete said. "I don't even know who Manabozho is, let alone anything about his tepee."

"'Manabozho's Tepee' is another name for Sugar Loaf Rock," Dan said. "It's the oldest of all the Indian legends."

"What will we be looking for?" Pete asked.

"I'm not sure," Dan replied, "but whatever it is won't be in plain sight. Sugar Loaf Rock gets climbed on, over, and through by thousands of tourists every year. Whatever it is that Lemuel Fisher put there, it has to be hidden pretty well."

"Right," Eddie said, getting up. "I'll round up some shovels from the horse barn."

"Okay, Eddie," Dan said, "I'll get some flashlights."

"Flashlights?" Pete asked. "How far down are you planning on digging?"

"I'm not planning on digging at all," Dan smiled. "Everybody ready? Let's go."

"You're going into the cave?"

CHAPTER 23
DAY 7   SUGAR LOAF ROCK

"Now, what?" Eddie asked, carrying a shovel toward Sugar Loaf Rock. "The ground looks pretty hard. I don't think we can dig two inches anywhere around here."

"You're right," Dan said, "I'm going to see what I can find with this flashlight." He pointed to a black hole about halfway up the northeast side of the rock.

"You're going into that cave?" Eddie asked. "I heard that people have gotten stuck in there and never come out."

"Yes," Dan said, "but I know there's a way. It's not something you try on your own. I'll need your help."

"Sounds to me," Pete said, "like it's not something you try at all. Do you know anyone who's done it?"

"No, but I've read about it in the *Town Crier*. Well, who's coming with me?"

"Are you sure you don't just want to dig some holes?" Eddie asked.

"Yes, I'm sure," Dan said, smiling. He turned and scrambled up the side of the limestone formation. The others followed and, in minutes, all four had reached the cave entrance.

119

"It looks a lot bigger from here than it did from down there," Pete said, joining the other three inside.

"That's why I brought some twine to tie around my waist," Dan said, handing the ball of string to his sister. "In case I get stuck, I can just turn around and follow the string out."

Everyone nodded but no one seemed as convinced as Dan that his idea was a very good one.

Dan tied the string around his waist, clicked on his flashlight, and stepped into the cave. In moments he had disappeared. The others peered inside and saw the light flickering on the walls. Kate held the ball of twine as it unraveled. After several minutes, it stopped.

"Are you okay?" Eddie yelled in.

"I'm not sure," Dan answered. He sounded like he was a mile away. "I've come to a dead end. I'm going to back up. Pull on the string, Kate, so I can tell which way to turn."

"Okay, Dan," Kate said. She tugged gently at the ball of twine. "I'll keep it just tight . . ."

"What happened?" Dan yelled. "I don't feel it anymore."

"It broke," Kate replied anxiously. "Are you still stuck? Can you turn around?"

"I'll try, but it's pretty tight in here," Dan called out. "No, I'm wedged in solid. I can't even turn enough to point the flashlight behind me. One of you will have to come in and get me."

Pete looked at Eddie, who, at the least, was twice the size of Dan. He glanced at Kate. Pete was even thinner than she.

"I'll go," Pete said. "How much more string do you have, Kate?"

"Plenty. I'll tie it around your ankle instead of your waist like we did with Dan. Here's the other flashlight."

Pete stepped cautiously into the cave. "I'm coming, Dan," Pete yelled. Pete worked his way to the left where the passage quickly narrowed to a squeeze. He looked to his right, grabbed a handhold and pulled himself onto a ledge. He took two more steps and wriggled his way through another crack into an open space. He aimed his light high, low, and in all directions—including behind him. Were it not for the string trailing from his ankle he would have no idea how to get back.

He turned and looked ahead. There, a few feet in front of him, was a narrow gap. Pete slipped through it and turned into another open area. He stood up and shined the light to the top of a high cavern. He judged that it almost reached the top of Sugar Loaf Rock. He trained the beam on a soft, velvety-looking object at the peak. After a few moments, the thing dropped from its position. Wings appeared. It was a huge bat. It flew directly toward Pete's face. Pete screamed and ducked as it darted toward him. The creature squealed and disappeared through a small crevice.

"Dan, can you hear me?" Pete yelled. "I'm getting shelled in here."

A moment later, Pete felt something on his shoulder. Instinctively, Pete spun around. He heard a click. A blazing light flashed in his eyes.

"Of course, I can hear you," Dan said casually with a wry grin.

"Dan? Hey, I thought you were stuck," Pete cried.

"Well, I was. Sort of. I couldn't think of a way to get you in here. I knew you wouldn't come unless things were pretty desperate, so I had to make you think I was going to die or something if you didn't come right away. I couldn't let you miss this. Look."

Dan flashed his light directly over his head into the catacomb.

"You mean all you wanted me to do was to come in here to get bombed by the bats?" Pete asked, more than a little annoyed.

"No," Dan said. He was still smiling. "You don't see what I'm showing you." Dan kept his light trained on a higher wall and his eye on Pete.

Pete turned his head in the direction of the beam. It caught the edge of an object about six feet over his head.

"I think that's what we're looking for," Dan said. "And I couldn't reach it on my own. I needed a boost."

"What is it?" Pete breathed.

"It's an old, black can," Dan said.

"A rusty tin can?" Pete scoffed. "If you're looking for old cans I can show you thousands of them at the dump behind my cottage."

"I didn't say tin," Dan continued, "and I didn't say rusty." His smile never changed. "I said black, as in tarnished. It is old, though. I'm guessing over fifty years old."

Pete glanced slowly back to the object still illuminated by the narrow beam of Dan's flashlight. It was metallic, and it was cylindrical, and it was black. But it was smooth and had a luster unlike anything Pete had ever seen, especially at the LaSalle Island dump. Its dull sheen was like his mom's old picture frame that held the tintype photo of his grandma and grandpa on their wedding day.

"You think this is the treasure?" Pete whispered.

"That's my guess," Dan answered calmly. "How about a boost?"

Pete leaned down and put his hands together forming a cup. "What are you waiting for?" Pete said anxiously. "Go get it."

Dan put his right foot in Pete's hands. Pete stood up raising Dan high into the cave.

Dan strained. "Just a couple more inches, Pete," he urged.

Pete stood up on his tip-toes.

"Got it," Dan said.

Pete set Dan down, and both of them examined the large cylinder with their flashlights. It was heavy for a can, but not heavy enough to hold much of a treasure. Dan shook it, and something rattled. It wasn't empty, but whatever was inside didn't clank like coins or jewels or anything. It thudded like a piece of cardboard or a folded-up paper. Dan checked the rim around the top and bottom. It was completely sealed.

"What do you think's in it?" Pete asked.

"I'm not sure, now. Another message, maybe," Dan answered. "Let's get out of here. Do you still have the string tied to you?"

"I guess," Pete said, checking for the cord on his ankle. "Yeah, I'm still on." He felt sort of like the trophy bass that had taken his lure into the weeds a couple of weeks before. Unlike the fish, however, Pete was glad he was still attached to the person on the other end.

"Are you guys okay?" Kate yelled.

"Yes," Dan answered. "We're coming out."

Pete took hold of the string. He trained his light on the narrow passageway ahead of him and followed the line back to the mouth of the cave. Pete's eyes had become accustomed to the weak beam of his small flashlight, so stepping out of the cavern, he was nearly blinded as he looked into the late morning sun. Kate grabbed him and planted a huge kiss right on his left cheek.

"You saved my brother, Pete," she said.

Pete blinked in surprise. He looked at Dan. Dan raised an eyebrow as if to say, "I won't tell on you if you don't tell on me."

"What did you guys find?" Eddie asked.

"A can," Dan said, winking to Pete.

"We think maybe there's a message in it," Pete said. He shook the canister so the others could hear the thump of the soft object inside.

"Are you sure it's not just a dead bat?" Eddie said with a laugh.

"Could be," Dan grinned.

"Let's get back to Aunt and Uncle's," Kate said, looking down the sheer wall of Sugar Loaf Rock. "We need a can opener."

"Mrs. Anderson and I will be visiting the Governor today."

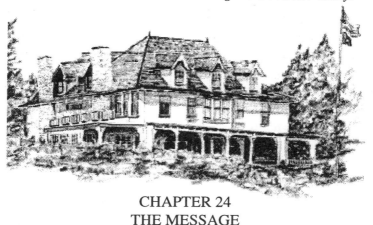

CHAPTER 24
THE MESSAGE

"Good morning," Nancy Anderson said as Kate led the three boys into the living room. "You were up and out early. Where did you go?"

"Sugar Loaf," Dan replied. "Do you know where a can opener is?"

"Daniel, Peter!" Mrs. Anderson exclaimed. "You two are positively filthy. What did you do, crawl through it?"

"Not quite," Dan replied. "We found what we were looking for about in the middle. That's why we need the can opener." He held out the blackened cylinder.

Nancy Anderson took one look and called up the stairway. "George, I think you'd better come down here."

"What's wrong, dear," Mr. Anderson called back.

"I'm not sure, but it looks as if the kids have one of General Fisher's silver canisters. They just found it at Sugar Loaf Rock."

"Coming." In seconds Mr. Anderson was down the stairs and standing in the living room beside the four teenagers. "How'd you find it?" he asked, turning the cylinder in his hands.

"Pete cracked the code in General Fisher's poem this morning," Dan said. "It led us to the cave at Sugar Loaf. It was way up on a ledge. We think General Fisher left a treasure, and this might be it. We're going to give whatever's inside to Edna, but my guess is, by the weight of it, that it's just a message of some kind."

"Edna's not doing very well," Kate added. "Especially now that her nephew, Ronald, is staying with her. There's been a lot of damage to her house lately. If this is another clue maybe it will lead us to the fortune that her father intended for her, and she'll be able to get back on her feet."

"That's a very noble cause," Mrs. Anderson said, walking toward the kitchen. "I'll bring a can opener. We'll all see what's inside together." In moments she returned.

"Pete," Dan said, "since you figured out the riddle in the poem, you should be the one to open the can."

"All right," Pete said, taking the cylinder, "but I hope, if it's a clue, that it won't be as hard to figure out as the last one."

He wheeled the opener around, and the lid popped up. Pete reached inside and lifted out a folded sheet of parchment. He unfolded it revealing one, four-line verse. He read aloud,

"'From Wigwam's dark den to the Isles of the
    Chenos,
Midsummer's morn under Ile aux Outardes,
'Neath a cairn and a cross will my progeny find
Aurum replete of the Mackinac bard.'"

"What in the world is that supposed to mean?" Eddie asked.

"'The Isles of the Chenos?'" Kate said, shaking her head. "It sounds like some place in China."

"And 'Wigwam's dark den?'" Pete asked "There are hundreds of Indian camps around here. Every one of them has dozens of wigwams. It could be any of them."

"'*Ile aux Outardes*?'" Eddie wrinkled his nose. "Must be some French place."

"Here we go again," Pete said, shaking his head. "We're no closer than we were before."

"Well, you kids have fun," George Anderson said, turning toward the front door. "And stay out of mischief. Mrs. Anderson and I are late for our visit with the Governor. We were just leaving when you came in."

"Zachary is preparing lunch for you right now," Mrs. Anderson said. "Go upstairs and freshen up. Especially you and Pete, Dan. I can't believe how dirty you two are."

George and Nancy Anderson left through the front door and walked down to the carriage that awaited them at the gate.

"Looks like it's back to the old Straits Room," Pete said.

"Sort of," Dan said, looking outside and watching his aunt and uncle step into the carriage. A smile crossed his face as Charles closed the landau's door. "Anyone up for a sail?"

"Sure, why?" Eddie asked.

"We just get a brand new, brain-buster of a clue to the treasure," Pete said, "and all you want to do is go for a sail?"

"Well, it won't be just any ordinary sail," Dan hinted.

"I've seen that look before," Kate said. "Don't tell me you've figured this thing out already."

Dan smiled. "Maybe. The last two lines are simple. It just says that he, Lemuel Fisher, the Mackinac Bard, has left for his children all his gold under a pile of stones with a cross on it. The toughest clues are in the first two lines. If I'm right though, they'll tell us exactly where to look."

"How do you figure?" Pete said, rereading the note. "It all sounds like mumbo-jumbo to me." Eddie and Kate nodded.

"Don't any of you remember the page in Mr. Dufina's book that showed the first map ever made of the Straits area? It was drawn by Marquette, himself." The other three looked at each other and shrugged. "Well, I do," Dan continued. "It had a group of islands listed as `Iles des Chenos' roughly where the Snows are. And then it hit me. 'Chenos' must be an old spelling for 'Cheneaux.'"

"The Snows?" Eddie gasped. "You mean the treasure is in the Snows?"

"Well, that narrows it down some," Pete said, "but the Les Cheneaux Islands is still a pretty big area to be looking for a pile of sticks and stones."

"Yes," Eddie agreed and looked to Dan. "Any idea on where to start?"

"You've been to French restaurants, haven't you, Eddie?" Dan said confidently.

"Sure," Eddie said. "What of it?"

"Well, my mom and dad like to take us to the Islington Hotel. They have a terrific French chef," Dan said, lifting an eyebrow. "My favorite dish is *flambe aux outardes*," he continued, pointing to the second line of the poem.

"*Flambe aux outardes*? Flaming goose?" Eddie asked.

"You're worse than General Fisher," Pete said. "What are you talking about?"

"I get it," Kate whispered. "*Ile Aux Outardes*. That's French for Goose Island!"

"Hey, Kate, you're right," Eddie said. "I remember seeing that in the chapter about Alexander Henry, the British guy who watched the massacre at Michilimackinac. *Ile aux Outardes* is where he finally escaped from the Ojibways."

"But Goose Island is a mile long and a quarter of a mile across," Kate said, shaking her head.

"That's right," Dan said. "But there's more to the clue. Remember that Indian legend about Manabozho, the guy Pete dreamed about? The Ojibways believe that Manabozho, the first man, was created by the Great Spirit, Gitchee Manitou, and sent here to Michilimackinac, the Land of the Great Dancing Spirits. Manabozho beached his canoe at the Giant's Stairway and made a pledge to the Great Spirit every step of the way as he walked up onto the Island. He went through Arch Rock straight to his tepee, or 'Wigwam,' which was Sugar Loaf Rock."

"It's only an old myth," Pete laughed. "You don't believe that, do you?"

"It doesn't matter," Dan replied.

"Okay, so what does it have to do with the treasure?" Pete asked.

"The cave, or 'dark den' of Manabozho's Wigwam, is the next clue," Dan explained. "It lines us up to the exact point on Goose Island where the treasure is hidden. Now, all we have to do is find out what the angle of the sun is on Midsummer's Morning. That's the day of the year when the sun rises at its furthest point north. We take that angle and draw a line from the Wigwam to where it cuts through *Ile Aux Outardes*, Goose Island. When we get there we look for a pile of stones with a cross over it."

"The Coast Guard station!" Kate said anxiously. "I'll bet they've got the angle of every sunrise of the year."

"We'll stop there first on the way to the *Griffin*," Eddie said.

"What about lunch?" Pete asked. "I'm starved."

"You're always starved," Eddie laughed.

"All right," Dan agreed. "Let's feed Pete's tapeworm and then we can go."

"And shouldn't we tell someone?" Pete insisted. "Remember what happened the last time we sailed from Mackinac Island to the Snows? We nearly wiped out on, as I recall, Goose Island. Oh, sure. You must remember," Pete said, trying to make his point, "Goose Island is the one with the huge boulders all around it. The waves crashed into us all night long. The *Griffin* would have been toothpicks in five minutes if we hadn't lucked out."

"That was one in a million," Eddie argued. "That could never happen again."

"What? That we lived through it?" Pete agreed.

"Pete's right," Kate said to Eddie.

Pete heaved a sigh of relief. Finally, someone was listening to reason.

"We'll leave a message telling Aunt and Uncle that we might be late for dinner," Kate reassured Pete.

"That's it?" Pete cried. "We'll leave a message? Have you all lost your minds?"

"Come on, Pete," Kate grinned. "Nothing's going to happen."

Pete rubbed his eyes and shook his head. "Okay," he sighed. "I'm coming. We're all going to our deaths. But just to be sure, let's none of us forget our cement life jackets."

. . . the cannon went off at Fort Mackinac.

CHAPTER 25
THE SAIL TO THE CHENOS

The four were just walking into the U.S. Coast Guard station when a cannon went off at Fort Mackinac. Dan glanced from his watch to the Coast Guard flag pole. It was 1:30, and The Stars and Stripes flapped easily in the light breeze. The wind was from the northwest, and no warning flags flew from the yardarm. It would be an easy sail to Goose Island.

"Excuse me, mister," Kate said to the white-suited man at the desk. "Can you tell us where the sun came up this morning?"

"Yes, ma'am. I was on duty," he said. "It came up right over Sainte Anne's steeple."

"How about some other day?" Kate pursued.

"Excuse me?"

"Another day of the year," Kate repeated. "Can you tell us the angle it would rise some other day?"

"Sure," the man said, reaching for a thick book on his desk. "Which day?"

"Midsummer's morning," Eddie interrupted anxiously.

"When?" the man asked.

"Midsummer's morning," Eddie repeated. "You know, the longest day of the year."

"You kids aren't with some sort of cult, are you? Witches and such? If you are, you can just pick up your bat wings and eyes of newt and sail out of here."

"No, it's nothing like that," Kate smiled to the officer. "It's a sailing project—a class on navigation."

"Oh, okay," the man said, glancing warily at Eddie. He opened the book and thumbed through the pages. "Here we go. The sun should come up on June twenty-first bearing precisely twenty-three degrees and twenty seven minutes north of east."

"Got that Eddie?" Kate asked.

"Got it," Eddie said, scribbling on a piece of paper. "May we see your Straits chart?" Kate asked.

"I can't let you take it out of here," he replied, surprised at the teenagers' interest. "But you could look at it here if you want to."

Eddie unrolled the large map on a nearby desk, and Dan set a compass point directly over Sugar Loaf Rock. He ran a straight edge on a line bearing precisely twenty-three degrees, twenty-seven minutes north of east. It ran through the center of a small bay on the western coast of Goose Island about a third of the way south of the northernmost tip.

Eddie glanced up at Dan and Kate with a questioning stare. "What do you think?" he whispered.

"It fits," Kate whispered back.

". . . perfectly," Dan added, nodding his head.

"Nobody's asked me," Pete put in.

"Okay," Dan said. "What do you think?"

"I think this is nuts," Pete pleaded. "Christopher Columbus had a better idea of where he was going. Here you are, heading off into Lake Huron without any idea of what the weather will be—not telling anyone where we're going, when we'll be back—and who knows what all else you're forgetting."

The others stood for a moment considering Pete's warning.

"Pete's right. This is insane," Dan said as he stepped toward the door. He turned and smiled, "Last one to the *Griffin*'s a scurvy, old landlubber."

Kate and Eddie followed quickly.

"Come on," Eddie said, reaching back and tugging at Pete's arm. "Where's your sense of adventure?"

"Why does everybody always want to know where my sense of adventure is?" Pete said, plodding a few steps behind. "I don't have a sense of adventure. What I do have is a very strong will to live. And right now, it's telling me that what you're confusing for adventure is just plain stupidity."

"Agreed," Kate said, stepping back and grabbing Pete's other hand. "And the only reason I'm going along is because I know you'll take care of us." She smiled looking Pete square in the eye. "That's your part of this team, Pete. Without you, we'd never make it home."

Pete followed shaking his head. "I shouldn't need to remind you what happened to the first *Griffin* that came through here. It went down with all hands."

"That was over three hundred years ago," Eddie laughed.

"Yeah, well, maybe it's due to happen again," Pete warned.

———

"It's almost four o'clock," Kate said. "We're making pretty good time."

The bow of the *Griffin* pointed directly for the small, Goose Island bay. Sugar Loaf Rock behind them was still visible, and Dan was straining to see landfall ahead.

133

"Treasure Bay, captain!" Dan called. "It be a point off the starboard bow, as I reckon."

"Aye, and Treasure Bay it will be. Sure we'll be digging up bounteous riches, won't we, me hearties," Eddie said in his Long John Silver brogue. "I've a feeling in me bones, I have," he squinted at Pete.

Pete rolled his eyes. He'd heard this sort of banter before. The last time was a month ago when they'd barely escaped Harold Geetings' island. That was too close for Pete, and he had no reason to believe that this would turn out any better.

"Aye, sure it is," Eddie continued. "Our fine, wee ship'll be laden heavy with silver and gold, rubies and pearls, doubloons and pieces of eight, heh, heh."

"Sure, me lads," Dan joined in. "This 'ere's going to be a day to beat all days, it will, heh, heh."

Pete held a jib halyard and gazed out at Goose Island trying not to think of all the dangers that lie ahead. *What if the Griffin hit a shoal? She'd crack like a robin's egg and go down in minutes. What if a storm came up? A white squall would toss us around like a kite in March. What if . . .*

"Pete," Eddie yelled. "Let go the jib!"

Dan scurried across the deck and grabbed the line from Pete's hand. He jerked it from the cam cleat and the sail luffed in the breeze. The *Griffin* slowed from four to two knots as it approached the pebbly shoreline. The sailboat's hull ground to a halt over the sand and pebble beach.

"You'd best to be a-warnin' us afore ye drift off like that again, matey," Dan said. "Where was ye bound t' this time, the Barbary Coast?"

"Huh? Oh, sorry," Pete mumbled. "I guess I was thinking about something else."

"All ashore, ye scurvy lubbers," Eddie bellowed.

Dan, Kate, and Pete slid off the sun-drenched, *Griffin* deck into the cold, knee-deep water. Dan grabbed the bow line and pulled the nose of the *Griffin* onto the beach. Eddie lashed down the main sail, hopped into the water, and waded ashore.

It was almost six o'clock before they began their search.

"Let's start in the bay," Dan said. "It should be right here. I'll take the north shore. Eddie, you take the south. Kate, you and Pete can go inland working back and forth between us. Remember, we're looking for a cross and a pile of stones."

"What if the cross was made of wood?" Kate asked. "It's probably all rotted away by now."

"Right," Eddie said. "And with the ice, wind, and waves over all the years, the stone pile may be nothing more than a few rocks laying around."

The four set off fanning away from the *Griffin*. Together they scoured the area with Kate and Pete working their way deeper and deeper into the uninhabited island. Soon, Dan and Eddie began to get ahead of Pete and Kate who had more ground to cover as they fanned out.

"Let's split up," Kate suggested. "You take that side and I'll take this, okay?"

Pete agreed and they set off in opposite directions.

———

"Kate, Eddie, Pete!" Dan called. Dan shaded his eyes as he watched two people in an outboard approach the island. "Someone's coming," he called into the woods.

In minutes Eddie and Kate were at Dan's side straining to see who could be aboard the small boat.

"Kate, have you seen Pete?" Dan asked his sister.

"Not for a while," she replied. "I yelled for him when you called me, but he didn't answer. I hope he hasn't

135

slipped off into one of his daydreams. We may never find him."

"I knew we shouldn't have left him," Eddie said, staring into the bay. "Could it be the Coast Guard?"

"It's only 6:30," Kate said, checking her watch. "Aunt and Uncle wouldn't be worried about us yet. Besides, even Uncle George couldn't get the Coast Guard out here this fast."

"And that little outboard is no Coast Guard boat," Dan agreed.

"Someone in the bow is waving to us," Kate said. "It looks like Miss Martin."

"The librarian?" Eddie laughed. "You're kidding. See, Dan, I told you to return that Popeye comic book."

"And I hadn't even gotten to the spinach part," Dan laughed.

"Wait a minute," Kate said seriously. "Who's that with her?"

"I don't know," Eddie smiled. "But with that black suit and hat, it could be Wimpy."

"Well, lets help them ashore," Dan said, walking into the water. He waved to return Miss Martin's greeting.

The driver of the outboard cut the engine. He turned his face away as he tilted the propeller out of the water. Miss Martin threw the bow line to Dan, and the three of them pulled the small outboard onto the beach.

Suddenly, the man in the stern spun around. He leveled the barrel of his pistol toward the eyes of the three stunned teenagers.

"You've done a fine job, kids," the stranger said with a sinister stare. "I couldn't have done this without you."

Ronald pedalled past the Arnold Dock.

CHAPTER 26
THE SPY

Ronald Sawyer stood behind a tree near Sugar Loaf Rock and watched the second boy go into the cave. It was so nice of Mr. Pounders to let him use his big spyglass. He could see far away things with it. Ronald began to shake with excitement when the two boys came out of the cave with a large, black can. He watched as the four kids looked at it and then scrambled down the rock to their bikes. Ronald ran to his own shiny red bicycle, the one Aunt Edna had given him, and followed the four teenagers. He stayed behind them out of sight as they raced for the Anderson's summer home on the West Bluff. He ditched his bike behind some lilac bushes and hid waiting for the four teens to come out of the barn. Then, after they had crossed the back yard and gone inside, Ronald slipped into the crawl space under the house.

Once there, it was easy for him to follow their voices just above his head to where they stopped in the living room. For the last week, Ronald had spent more time here than he had at his Aunt Edna's place in the Annex. It was from here, just a few days ago, he had heard them talk about a big, blue book and how important it was to find the one that said Volume One on it. Then, only this morning, he had listened to them say that his grandpa's poem would show them the way to the treasure, and that a map told them that Sugar Loaf Rock was the place to find it. As soon as the room became quiet above him, he went into town and told Mr. Pounders at the pool hall everything he had heard.

Now, again, he was standing under the big house on the West Bluff directly beneath the four teenagers. He heard them say that the silver can they found at Sugar Loaf wasn't the treasure but only a clue to where they would find it. They talked about some place called the Chenos and about a special wigwam. He heard them say they were going to ask about some sunrise at the Coast Guard station and then they would sail off to Goose Island to get the General's Treasure. When he couldn't hear them talking any more he slipped back out from under the summer home and ran to his bicycle.

———

Mr. Pounders will be real glad to hear about this, Ronald thought as he pedaled past the Arnold Dock toward Horn's Bar. Ronald had been real good about doing all the things Mr. Pounders had told him to do. He was so lucky he had met Mr. Pounders. Mr. Pounders gave him candy every time he did something for him.

Mr. Pounders will be so happy when I tell him about the Chenos and how I followed the kids to the Coast Guard station. Mr. Pounders will give me a big piece of licorice. Now I'll get Grandpa's money. Mr. Pounders said I would. I'll get all the money and Aunt Edna won't get any. She would have kept it to herself if she found it. Mr. Pounders said so. Aunt Edna is so mean. She said she didn't even think there was any treasure.

So, she shouldn't get any of it, anyway. She didn't know anything.

Mr. Pounders had told Ronald how to steal the two books from the library when Miss Martin wasn't looking. And when Ronald got the big blue book from Aunt Edna's book shelf, Mr. Pounders had given him a whole bag of black licorice, his favorite kind. Mr. Pounders would have given him lots more if he had gotten Grandpa Fisher's poem. He had gone all the way to the third floor of the Anderson Cottage, but when he heard someone moving in one of the rooms, he became frightened. He sneaked back down the stairs and listened from under the house. Pretty soon he heard two of the boys right above him. They talked about a secret room on the third floor where they were going to hide the poem. Then one of them said he had seen a bike outside and wondered why it was there. *That must be my bike*, Ronald thought. In a panic, Ronald ran from under the house, grabbed his bike, and took off to tell Mr. Pounders about the secret room.

The next day he went back to the third floor of the Anderson House after he had followed the four kids to the Grand Hotel pool. He sneaked into the house and up the stairs, but he couldn't find any secret door, only four bedrooms and a linen closet. Mr. Pounders would have given him all the licorice in the world if he had gotten into the secret room. But now he watched them as they went into the Coast Guard station.

———

As soon as the girl led the three boys from the Coast Guard station to the marina, Ronald slipped out of his hiding place across Huron Street. He hurried up the stairs behind Horn's Bar. Mr. Pounders was hunched over a table playing a game of cards with his friends.

"Ronald, I told you not to bother me when I'm working," the squat, bleary-eyed man said. "Go away."

"But Mr. Pounders," Ronald pleaded, "the four kids are getting in their sailboat to go to Goose Island. They found out where Grandpa's treasure is."

Mr. Pounders jumped up knocking over the poker table. He glared from Ronald to the three men across from him. "You didn't hear that! Do you hear me! None of you heard that! Get out of here, all of you. One word of this and all three of you are dead. Do you understand? Dead!"

The three men skulked away slipping silently down the stairs.

"I told you, Ronald. Never do that!" Mr. Pounders yelled. "When you have something to tell me, you do it when I'm alone. Now, get the boat ready. Don't talk to anyone."

Ronald fled down the stairs. He'd never seen Mr. Pounders so mad. He got on his bike and rode along the east shore past Mission Point. He pulled off the road and hid his bike in the bushes where Mr. Pounders kept the outboard.

————

Jake Pounders grabbed his binoculars and looked from the pool hall window into the marina. He watched as the teenagers rigged their sailboat and got underway around the east breakwall. He hurried down the stairs, boarded his carriage, and went up to the library. In minutes he and Miss Martin were seated in the buckboard and on their way to meet Ronald.

Ronald had the fourteen foot Tomahawk outboard in the water when the unlikely-looking couple arrived. Jake Pounders was a dark, slug of a man, short and stumpy with greasy, black hair. He wore a thin, black moustache, black suit, and a wide-brimmed, black hat. Next to him was seated a very prim, bright-eyed, young woman wearing a flowery dress. She sat straight and tall and was clearly a lady of distinction. The two stepped quickly from the small carriage. Mr. Pounders tied the horse and buggy behind a nearby grove of trees. Ronald stood barefoot in the water holding the boat as the offshore breeze tugged it gently into the Straits.

"There they are," Ronald pointed to a sailboat disappearing over the horizon. "Did I do good, Mr. Pounders?"

"Yeah, Ronald, you did good," Mr. Pounders said with a sneer. "Okay, everybody, let's go for a little boat ride." As Ronald stepped into the bow of the outboard Hazel Martin saw Jake pull a pistol from inside his coat. He checked the ammunition clip and then slipped it back out of sight. "This is going to be fun," he smiled to Miss Martin. "A nice, tidy conclusion, don't you think, Hazel?"

Hazel Martin turned and looked into the distance at the white sail of the sloop.

"I've been waiting a long time for this," Mr. Pounders said, pushing the boat away from shore. "Twenty years I've known about the General's Treasure. Hundreds of people have come to Mackinac looking for it. They all left, one by one, empty-handed. All but me. I've holed up here summer and winter in that rat trap of a pool hall. I'd get a lead now and then, but all were blind alleys. I always knew the final answer was with that old bird, Edna Fisher, but I couldn't get close enough to even speak to her. And then Ronald came. I knew right away that he was my ticket into her house. It didn't take me long to draw him into my plan, but I'd never have gotten my big break without your help, Doll. Who'd have thought that a poem and an old book would hold the final clues?" Mr. Pounders talked in hushed tones to the lady at his side while Ronald watched the sailboat drifting off to the northeast.

"Mr. Pounders! Mr. Pounders!" Ronald said. "They're getting away! Hurry!"

"We wouldn't want to get too close, would we now, Ronald," Jake Pounders warned. "They might see us and lead us away from your treasure."

"Oh, that's right, Mr. Pounders. We don't want them to think we're following them to MY treasure, right?"

"That's right, Ronald," Mr. Pounders smirked.

Jake Pounders pulled the starting cord on the twenty-five horsepower, Kiekhaefer-Mercury engine. It roared into action and Mr. Pounders quickly turned the throttle to SLOW. He let it idle a moment and then put it into gear. The sleek, wooden-hulled outboard picked up speed and pulled away from Mackinac Island. Mr. Pounders knew that if he could keep just the top part of the sailboat's mast in sight, those aboard the sloop would be unable to see the lower outboard. With a fresh breeze and a broad reach, the sailboat flew ahead to the northeast. Mr. Pounders kept the throttle at half speed to stay just out of sight.

Finally, Mr. Pounders slowed the engine as the sailboat approached Goose Island. He waited in the distance keeping close enough to see the four teens wade ashore. He then reversed away from the island and cut the engine. All was quiet. Fifteen minutes passed as Mr. Pounders sat glancing at his watch. Finally, he looked up.

"I'm going to need your help here, Ronald," Mr. Pounders said. He pulled the cord to start the motor. The engine whined for a moment before Mr. Pounders turned the throttle to low idle. "I want you to stand up on the bow, Ronald. Wave your arms so those kids on shore can see you."

"Okay, Mr. Pounders," Ronald said. He jumped up on the bow and stood on the tips of his toes. Try as he may, though, he couldn't see the kids—only the very top of their sailboat and the Goose Island trees.

"I don't think they can see me," he said turning to Mr. Pounders.

Mr. Pounders reached back and slipped the gear to reverse. He gunned the throttle and the water churned.

"No!" screamed Hazel Martin.

Ronald lurched forward and splashed into the frigid Lake Huron water. "Help," he yelled. "I can't swim."

"Oh, that's awful, Ronald," Mr. Pounders laughed. "I guess this might be a good time to learn." He spun the tiller, pulled the gear forward, and cranked the throttle to full speed. He swerved past the floundering Ronald Sawyer and flew toward Goose Island. Jake Pounders kept his eye on the small bay in front of him while Miss Martin watched Ronald thrash frantically in the water. Soon, Ronald was beyond her sight. She turned and focused on the beached sailboat, her soft features hardening in a fixed stare.

As the outboard entered the shallow water, Mr. Pounders slowed the engine. "Lean over the bow and watch for rocks," he instructed the librarian. "We wouldn't want a busted prop to get between us and a fortune."

The small boat weaved its way around several large boulders that lay in the shallow waters. "Look," Jake Pounders said as he pointed toward the beach, "they see us. Wave for them to pull us ashore."

"Dan! Kate! Eddie!" Hazel Martin yelled. "Give us a hand."

"Good," Jake Pounders said, slipping the red and silver Mercury into neutral. "Where's the fourth one," he growled. "Didn't Ronald say that there were four of them?"

"I didn't hear him say anything at all," the librarian replied. "But there was another boy with them when they came to the library the other day."

"I can't wait any longer," Jake snarled. "I'd like to get all four of them at once, but I think they're getting wise. Just keep smiling at them, Doll. Don't lose their attention. Say something."

"I'm so glad to see you," Hazel yelled, throwing the bow line toward Dan. "Where's your friend? Didn't he come with you?"

Something was fishy. Dan could feel it. He could almost smell it. Why was Miss Martin out in a small outboard this far from Mackinac Island? And who was this character in the black suit? *It's not Ronald, but who could he be? He's built enough like him.* "Pete's in the woods," Dan called back to Miss Martin. "What brings you to Goose Island?" *I wonder if this is the guy we saw from the South American that day?* Dan thought. *He couldn't be Miss Martin's boyfriend, could he? I wonder if he's the one that's been following us around.*

Just then Jake Pounders spun in his seat and pulled the gun from his shoulder holster. He smiled as he leveled it directly into Dan's eyes. "You've done a fine job, kids. I couldn't have done this without you."

Somehow they had gotten the final piece to the treasure puzzle.

CHAPTER 27
TERROR

Kate, Dan, and Eddie froze.

All three knew at once that the man and woman before them were behind all the destruction at Edna Fisher's cottage in the Annex. Somehow, they had gotten the final piece to the treasure puzzle. They also knew that there was nothing they wouldn't do now that General Fisher's gold was within their reach. The kids also knew that Pete was their only hope to get them out of this mess. It would be just their luck that he was having another one of his catatonic daydreams. And when he came out of it, he'd probably stumble right into the center of them with a big, "Howdy, Miss Martin. What brings you here?"

The three glanced nervously at each other. How could this be? Miss Martin, the straight-laced librarian, involved in any way with this slimeball, pool hall character? But when they thought about it, it all fell into place. She must have been in on this from the very beginning. Miss Martin had missed her calling. She should have been in Hollywood. No wonder she was so interested in General Fisher's poem. And that's how they were putting the clues

145

together ahead of them—she had copied the entire poem that day at the library. She even closed early that morning so she could run off and tell her creepy boyfriend that the kids had found the poem and what it had meant. Then she must have taken the set of *Historic Mackinac* books from the library shelves so the kids couldn't use them. That's how she knew it was a two-volume set. She had taken them herself! And Jake Pounders must have done at least some of the damage to Edna Fisher's cottage—probably even started the fire that would have burned the house down if Dan and Kate hadn't had their dreams. He was the guy they had seen from the *South American*.

"Okay, on your faces," Mr. Pounders ordered. "Miss Martin, here, she's going to keep you from wandering about. I've got some plans for each of you. Here's some rope, Doll. Let's see how good you are at tying knots." Mr. Pounders tossed a length of anchor line to her. She caught it and went to work. Mr. Pounders shoved the barrel of his gun into Eddie's ear. "You first, on your belly."

Eddie fell onto the pebbles of the shoreline. Miss Martin wrapped the rope three times around his wrists and then pulled his ankles together with two half-hitches.

"Now, you," he said to Dan. Dan knelt down and the librarian clamped his arms behind him. Mr. Pounders pushed his head to the beach and Miss Martin ran several more loops around his legs.

"You're next, Blondie," Mr. Pounders sneered at Kate.

"Why don't you just kill us now," Kate yelled. "You're going to do it anyway, right? Or are you too weak to do it in cold blood?"

"Kate!" Eddie whispered.

"Well, you are, aren't you?" Kate said, looking up at the man who stood before her. All the while, Hazel Martin wrapped a line around Kate's wrists. She took a couple of wraps around Kate's mouth to shut her up. Then she tied Kate's legs together. The three Cincinnati Row teenagers wriggled helplessly on the beach.

"I'm keeping you alive," Mr. Pounders smiled, "in case my metal detector here doesn't find what I think it's going to find. Plus, I need some bait to catch your lost little friend." From the bow of the outboard he brought a long, metallic device wrapped in a black cloth. He turned the switch and the instrument buzzed. Mr. Pounders began walking the beach. "So, we're looking for a cross and a pile of stones?" he said as he kicked Eddie in the ribs.

"How'd you know about that?" Eddie winced.

"You might say I heard it from a little birdie," Mr. Pounders smirked as he moved the metal detector around the area. "Or to be exact, an overgrown mole. I believe you've met Ronald Sawyer? It seems he's been spending a good deal of his time under the Anderson's living room for the past week. He's gone now, had a little swimming accident. But just before he died, he told me some very interesting things about the General's Treasure. He said that the clue you found this morning at Sugar Loaf told you exactly where to find the treasure. Now, I'm going to give each of you one chance. Where is it?"

Mr. Pounders stood next to Eddie. Eddie groaned as Mr. Pounders dug the toe of his boot deep into his ribs.

"I didn't find it," Eddie pleaded. "Honest!"

"Then you won't be any help to me," Mr. Pounders said. He grabbed Eddie by the nape of the neck, untied his legs, and marched him out of sight behind a stand of birch trees. Moments later Dan and Kate heard the explosion of a gunshot.

The twins lay on the ground shaking, terror stricken, as Mr. Pounders returned alone, smoke coming from his gun.

"Now, you, wise guy," Mr. Pounders said. "Maybe you know something you were keeping from your friend."

Dan stood, ghost white, his knees twitching. He gasped for breath as Mr. Pounders pressed the barrel of the pistol into the base of his skull.

"Yes," Dan lied. "I might have found it. There were some stones in the woods. A little way from here."

"This better be good," Mr. Pounders growled. "Or you won't go as quick as your friend."

In minutes, another shot rang out. Again a single set of footsteps made its way back to camp.

Kate was in hysterics. Inconsolable. Mr. Pounders approached. Miss Martin stood above her. "Now, Sweetheart," he sneered. "Get up."

Miss Martin loosened the ankle ropes and Kate struggled to her feet. She was limp with fear and shaking uncontrollably.

Just then, from out of the woods, Pete walked into the clearing carrying a heavy, black cylinder.

I've got to show Kate. This is the most beautiful place I've ever seen.

CHAPTER 28
EUREKA!

Pete had started out with Kate working the area between Dan and Eddie. They scoured the land for anything that might resemble a hill of rocks or a wooden cross. Kate noticed, as they went deeper into the island, that Dan and Eddie were getting ahead of them. "Let's split up," she suggested to Pete.

"Fine by me," Pete said. "Yell if you find something."

"You'll hear me," Kate laughed, and the two set off in opposite directions.

As Pete combed the eastern part of the narrow island, he soon lost sight of Kate as she covered the western half. Pete glanced around and found himself in a serene hollow. Moist, lichen-covered rocks and a dense canopy of foliage provided a cool, green setting like an outdoor sanctuary. The steady crashing of Lake Huron rollers breaking on the beach were muted by the lush barrier of trees and bushes. Only the twittering of small songbirds among the branches broke the stillness of the outdoor chapel. Pete looked around in awe of the setting's simple splendor. *I'll bet no one has ever been here before*, Pete thought.

I've got to find Kate. This is the prettiest place I've ever seen. It reminded him of the small grove on LaSalle Island near Government Bay. He thought about the time a few years before that he and his sister had seen a bear splashing in the shallow water ahead of them as they walked the trail.

A firecracker went off in the distance. Pete blinked and shook his head. *Oh, no, I've done it again*, he thought. The sunlight was not nearly as strong as it had been. *They're ready to leave and can't find me, so they're setting off cherry bombs to get me to come back.*

Pete turned to go in the direction of the loud noise and was stepping over a fallen birch when he looked to his left. A pile of stones set amid a green, mossy area caught his eye. In the middle were two mildewed, wooden boards. In a flash, he recognized it as the scene in Edna Fisher's oil painting, the one that had fallen to the floor the night of the dinner in the Annex. It was the picture that had the poem tucked in the frame. His eyes widened. With his next step, he stubbed his toe and fell flat on his face. He scrambled to his feet. *This is it*, he thought. *That picture at Edna's place was the General's final clue—so that's what 'The Place' meant on the frame. It all fits. Alexa's husband must have gotten Lemuel's message and thought it pointed to Bois Blanc. That's why he lived there, trying to find 'The Place,' and all the time it was here on Goose Island.*

Pete rushed to the stone cairn. He rolled twenty or thirty softball-sized rocks to the side. As he lifted the last of them, the edge of a tarnished cylinder came into view. It was exactly the same size as the one Dan had found at Sugar Loaf. He dug the dirt away with his fingers. He tried to wiggle it loose. It wouldn't budge. He stood up and took a hold with both hands and tugged for all he was worth. It was as if it had been cemented into place. He dropped to his knees once again and clawed at the black soil. Soon he had exposed a cylinder almost the length of Dan's, and still it wouldn't move. Pete put both of his hands together and pulled it toward him. The black can snapped loose and Pete flew backwards. He picked it up. It was a lot heavier than the one at Sugar Loaf. He glanced back at the hole. Looking in, he saw the tops of five others just like it. He could see that they had been placed so that all would be exposed when the first was discovered. He sprang to his feet. He would find Kate and show her. He picked up the cylinder. It weighed a ton. With both hands he could barely lift it. It must have been made out of pure gravity.

Another firecracker went off. Pete looked through the trees in the direction of the blast. It was getting dark. *They must be really worried. I can hardly wait to show them,* Pete thought. *I bet their eyes will come right out of their heads.*

Pete struggled back along the trail of broken branches. He could see the shore where the *Griffin* was beached. A few feet from the sailboat an outboard was pulled up on shore. He looked into the clearing and saw Kate. A woman stood next to her. *It's Miss Martin, the librarian. She's going to be thrilled to see this,* Pete thought. *Gee, I wonder what she's doing here.* Pete stepped ahead from behind a large, leafy maple tree.

"Hi, Miss Martin," Pete said. "Kate, look at . . ." In an instant he noticed the ropes on Kate's hands. Off to the side was a man wearing a black suit. Pete froze as the visitor pulled a gun from his shoulder holster. Pete glanced back at Kate. She was trembling in panic and tears were pouring from her eyes. Dan and Eddie were nowhere around. The loud noises Pete had heard weren't firecrack-

151

ers. They were gun shots. Dan and Eddie were dead and he was about to be next.

The man leveled the pistol at Pete's head and took one step toward him. Pete blinked and ducked as the gun fired. The metal can in Pete's hands chinged. Pete fell backward from the force of the bullet. He dropped the can and scrambled to his feet. The man took another step toward him and slipped on a rock. The gunman went down in a heap.

Before the man could get up Pete had turned and was crashing through the dense underbrush. In a moment, he had disappeared from sight.

Maybe I could sneak back and take the outboard for help.

CHAPTER 29
FLIGHT

"Come back here," Mr. Pounders yelled. "Now! Or I'll blow your pretty friend's head off."

Pete stopped cold. The thought flashed through his head of Kate being shot right then unless he turned around and gave himself up. *He wouldn't let Kate go. He's already killed Dan and Eddie. Kate's only chance now is if I can get away. I've got to get off this island. That outboard on the beach—if I could get him to follow me away from it I might be able to sneak back and take it to Mackinac for help.*

Pete watched from behind a tree. The sun had set. When he saw the man in the distance, he picked up a stone and took aim. Pete threw it so that it would land in the water with a splash. Mr. Pounders grabbed Miss Martin and Kate and ran toward the sound. Pete hurried through the woods and found another stone. He tossed that into the water, and the man rushed ahead. Pete drew the man closer and closer to the end of the island.

At the southernmost point Pete stood hidden by a clump of birches. It was nearly dark. He remembered what

Eddie had said about this place. This is where Alexander Henry made his final escape from the Ojibways after Pontiac's Massacre. Pete remembered the terrifying story in the blue book that told how all the British soldiers had been murdered, and the Indians had drunk their blood. Pete stood and stared blankly into Lake Huron. *Hold it,* Pete thought. *I can't be having a daydream now. Kate's only chance is for me to stay on my toes. Come on. Wake up.* Pete turned and saw Mr. Pounders pushing Kate and Miss Martin toward him. Pete spun toward the north. He slipped out of the forest onto the beach and ran until the man again was out of range.

As Pete hurried along the shoreline he got to wondering why Mr. Pounders was keeping both Kate and Miss Martin with him as he was chasing Pete. That had to slow him down. It made sense that he'd keep Kate with him— sort of as a hostage to get Pete. But why was Miss Martin tagging along? She must be in cahoots with Mr. Pounders, or why would she be on the island at all? But, if they were partners, why wasn't she back guarding the boats? Something wasn't adding up. Then it dawned on him. Maybe Miss Martin's not in with Mr. Pounders at all. Maybe she's like Kate, and he's using both of them to get the treasure.

The moon was just coming up and it became easier for Pete to see the outline of the trees as he raced to the outboard. He had almost gotten there when he glanced ahead. As he took his eye off the ground he tripped over something that lay on the beach.

"Ugh," he heard beneath him as he tumbled forward onto the sand.

"*Ugh?*" Pete thought. *Roots and rocks, when you trip over them, don't go, 'Ugh.'* He pulled the penlight from his pocket. Laying face down in front of him was the shape of a person. Pete shined the light at its head. It was Eddie! Eddie's mouth, hands, and feet were bound in anchor rope. His muffled moans urged Pete to free him. "Eddie! Are you okay?" Pete whispered as he rolled him over.

Eddie nodded, his eyes flashing in terror. Pete reached in his other pocket and took out his fishing knife. He flicked it open and slit the ropes. "Where's Dan?" Pete asked.

"I don't know," Eddie panted. "Mr. Pounders brought me here and stuck his gun right next to my ear. He pulled the trigger and the explosion was louder than anything I've ever heard in all my life. I thought I was dead. The next thing I heard was Mr. Pounders laughing as he was tying me up. Either his gun's loaded with blanks and he doesn't know it, or he's got something worse up his sleeve than just killing us. Either way, I don't like our chances of getting off this island alive."

"If he wanted to kill you," Pete said, closing his knife, "he wouldn't have tied and gagged you. And he's not shooting blanks. If I hadn't been carrying one of the silver cans when he shot at me, I'd have been a goner."

"A silver can?" Eddie asked. "You found the treasure?"

"Yeah, back there in the woods," Pete sighed.

From a distance, Pete and Eddie heard a voice.

"Nice trick, you little wart," Jake Pounders yelled. "But it didn't work, so you might as well give it up." His voice was coming from the camp where the *Griffin* and the outboard were beached. "I'm sitting right here between the two boats and you're not going anywhere. Now, get over here before I start putting holes in this pretty little girl's face!"

"I'm too late," Pete moaned.

"Too late for what?" Eddie asked.

155

"I thought I could get to the outboard before he got back from the other end of the island. But now, at least, it's two against one. Maybe we can figure out how to surprise him and get his gun away."

"Don't you mean two against two?" Eddie corrected. "Don't forget that two-faced librarian."

"I don't think Miss Martin's in with him, Eddie," Pete said. "No more than Kate is. I think he's been using her, too."

"Well, maybe," Eddie whispered, "but I wouldn't count on her to help."

Mr. Pounders had started a fire on the beach between the two boats. It glowed in the night and blew bright ashes into the sky.

"It's going to get cold pretty soon, Boy," he called out. "There's no way off this island, so you may as well come in now."

Pete and Eddie crept around the shoreline keeping Mr. Pounders in view but staying out of sight behind the trees and shrubs. As they moved silently along the shore, Pete, once again, stubbed his toe on something beneath him. He nearly cried out in pain before turning and seeing the outline of another person laying in the shadows. Could it be Dan? Pete flicked his light on the quivering figure before him. It WAS Dan! He handed the light to Eddie and put his knife to work on the ropes. Pete quickly freed Dan's hands and legs while Eddie untied the gag from his mouth. The three of them knelt in the sand looking at each other, mixed feelings of terror, relief, and joy overcoming them. The three hid behind a boulder as they talked about what they should do.

"Okay," Pete said, "he's not expecting all three of us, only me. I think we can take him if we charge from different directions all at once."

"Let's do it," Eddie said.

"Whatever we try, we've got to do it now," Dan said. "This guy's crazy. He could turn that gun on Kate any second."

They split up and sneaked toward the campfire, Pete from the north, Eddie from the south, and Dan from the east. Each crouched low and crawled into place ten yards from the bonfire. Pete gave a whistle and each raced towards Mr. Pounders. As they converged, Mr. Pounders leaped back from his place near the fire. All at once, Dan, Pete, and Eddie tripped on a wire and fell on their faces at Mr. Pounders' feet. A moment later an explosion went off. The three boys looked up to see Jake Pounders standing over them holding a smoking gun to Kate's head. Kate's eyes rolled back. She had fainted dead away.

"Well, isn't this a pleasant surprise," Jake Pounders said, staring at Pete. "I knew I'd get you if I kept your three little friends for bait." Miss Martin sobbed as she knelt on the ground with her face buried in her hands. "Now that you're all here," Jake continued, "and I've got the treasure, I guess all that's left is to get rid of all you spectators." Mr. Pounders let go of Kate and she slumped to the ground in front of Pete. Jake reached down and hoisted the silver cylinder into the air. A gold coin trickled out of a gaping hole and dropped onto the sand. "So, if you'll excuse me, I have a new life to live. It's a pity none of you will be around to share it with me. Especially you, Hazel. We could have had such a good time. You didn't really think I was going to share this with you, did you, my dear?"

"Not for a minute," Hazel Martin said, flashing a stare of hatred toward the small, swarthy man. "And I never wanted it. If you didn't have Dan and Kate constantly in your sights and weren't threatening to kill Edna Fisher, I would have turned you in a long time ago. When I found out that it was you that made Ronald steal General Fisher's old books I knew you wouldn't stop there. You know what you are, Jake Pounders? You're scum. And do you know what else? There's no amount of money on this earth that will make you any less miserable than you already are."

"Yeah, well, we'll see about that," Jake Pounders smirked. His eyes tightened and a cheerless grin crossed his lips. "Too bad none of you will be around to witness my agony." He checked his revolver. Five cartridges remained in the chambers, one for each of his captives. Mr. Pounders looked down at the five people lying at his feet. He noticed an odd expression on each of their faces. It wasn't the look of fear as he expected, but one more of surprise or even hope. They weren't staring right at him, either, but sort of past him. Something or someone was coming up from behind.

Mr. Pounders turned slowly. In the reddish glow of the campfire, he saw the shape of a small, roundish figure standing two feet behind him. Water dripped from his hair and face and clothes. The man strained under the weight of a massive boulder poised high over his head. In the red firelight Jake Pounders' arrogant smile changed instantly to an expression of shock. The small, muscular man made a low, guttural grunt and brought the tremendous rock crashing toward Jake Pounders' head. Mr. Pounders threw his hands in front of his face. His gun flew into the air. The boulder grazed his skull and crashed heavily onto his shoulder. Jake Pounders teetered for a moment. His knees buckled, and he went down like the curtain on a two-bit show.

Pete seized the gun and pointed it at Mr. Pounders. Jake lay writhing in the sand, blood gushing from his temple and an egg-sized bulge erupting from his skull.

"Get a rope, Dan," Pete said. Dan untied Kate and lashed the rope to the man groveling on the ground before him.

"I'm so sorry I doubted you," Kate said, rushing to Miss Martin. "Please forgive me."

"You had every right to think what you did," Hazel Martin said, breaking into tears. "I must take some blame. I was so angry when Mr. Pounders stole the library's books that I put all of our lives at risk in order to get them back. I was sure that I could handle him, but I was wrong. He got the best of me."

Kate turned to Ronald Sawyer as he lay sobbing in the sand. She went to him and held his hand.

"He lied to me," Ronald cried. "He wasn't my friend. He didn't like me at all. He tried to drown me."

"Well, you got back at him, Ronald," Kate said. "You stopped him from stealing General Fisher's treasure, and you saved all of our lives. You're a hero, Ronald."

"Eddie, follow me," Pete said, handing the gun to Dan. "Hold the fort, Dan. We'll be right back." Eddie followed Pete into the woods. Two minutes later, they returned. Pete struggled under the weight of two silver canisters as he walked over to Ronald Sawyer.

"Things will be better for you soon, Ronald," Pete said as he set the cans on the beach. Eddie followed Pete out of the woods carrying three more cylinders. "When your aunt gets these, Ronald," Pete continued, "she'll make sure you get the kind of help you need. She really does love you."

A flash of light from an off-shore search beam caught everyone's attention. A boat was approaching from the general direction of Mackinac Island.

"Someone's coming," Pete called out. "Get into the woods, quick. It could be some of Jake's buddies!"

159

A powerful search beam aboard the approaching boat penetrated the night. It flashed along the Goose Island shoreline and homed in on the bonfire between the two boats. The low hum of a large engine droned softly as it eased its way along the rocky coast. Pete could see the outlines of several people standing in the open craft. He began to hear the voices of those aboard. The boat moved in closer to the nervous teens until the beacon reflected enough light for Pete to see the people on its forward deck. Along with two Coast Guardsmen and a policeman, Pete saw the Andersons and Edna Fisher looking toward the dark shore.

"It's Aunt and Uncle!" Kate screamed.

The four teens jumped out of the bushes and waved for joy.

"This is the last treasure I ever want to see."

CHAPTER 30
REWARD

"Is everyone all right?" George Anderson called out as the boat drifted onto the beach.

"We're okay, now," Dan said.

"What in the world is going on?" Nancy asked.

"Well," Kate began, "it's a long story." Then she explained what had happened since they had last seen the Andersons that morning and how Jake Pounders had tricked everyone and was about to kill all of them.

"Oh, how dreadful," Nancy Anderson exclaimed.

"When you didn't get home for dinner," George Anderson said, "we became very concerned. We couldn't think of where you might be. But then your Aunt Nancy remembered the clue that you had found in the can, so we called Edna Fisher. She told us that her nephew was missing, too, so then we became really worried. Edna told us that the only person Ronald had ever mentioned was the pool hall owner, so we went there. It was locked and no one was inside. Then Charles took us to the marina. We found that the *Griffin* was out of her slip. We hurried to the Coast Guard station and asked the man on duty if he knew anything about four kids on a sailboat. He said that some teenagers had come by earlier. They had asked for the direction of sunrise on midsummer's morning and then he saw them point to Goose Island on his chart. We figured that you must have come here to look for the treasure. The only reason we came was because we were worried that you might have run aground here on Goose Island."

"Well, you would have found us, all right" Dan said. "But we wouldn't have been alive. Not if Pete hadn't gone into one of his brain breaks."

"Don't let anyone ever tell you not to have daydreams, Pete," Kate said as she held his hands in hers. "This time it saved our lives."

"At least I know when it's happening now," Pete said blushing. "And how to come out of it."

The policeman jumped from the bow of the Coast Guard boat and hurried over to Mr. Pounders who was holding his head and writhing on the beach.

Next, Edna Fisher stepped from the boat and ran to Ronald. "Oh, Ronald," Edna said. "I was so worried."

Ronald threw his arms around her. "I'm sorry, Aunt Edna. I won't ever be bad again. I cross my heart."

"We'd better get back to Mackinac and call your parents," George Anderson said, reaching out to help Kate aboard. "When we put the clues together, we called your mother and father. We wanted them to know that you were safe. We had no idea at that time how much danger you were in."

The policeman took his handcuffs from his belt. "What's in the cans," he asked, stepping towards Jake Pounders.

"The only one that's open is the one that stopped Mr. Pounders' bullet," Pete said holding a gold coin. "It cut a hole just big enough for some of these to come out."

162

Mr. Anderson looked carefully as he aimed his flashlight on two of the coins. "They're both 1881, twenty dollar gold pieces," he said, letting out a whistle. "Each one is worth probably five hundred dollars. There may be six hundred in each can."

"It's your inheritance, Miss Fisher," Pete said. "The General's Treasure. All six cans."

"Land sakes alive," she said in astonishment. "That's nearly two million dollars. I'll never need all that. We'll have to share. If it weren't for you four, I would have nothing. You saved my boat, my house, even my life. Then you risked your own lives finding my father's treasure. No, I wouldn't think of keeping all this to myself. There are six cans, you say? Each of you should get your own can for your part of the reward. I'll keep one for Ronald and one for myself. You get to pick first, Pete. Which one would you like?"

"Really?" Pete gasped.

"Yes, really," Edna said. "I'm sure my father would have wanted the people who were able to solve his riddle to have it."

"Well, I suppose, when you put it that way—I guess I'd like to keep the can that saved my life," Pete said, lifting the canister with the hole in the center. "And I hope it's the last treasure I ever see."

"I think we'd better get back to Mackinac," Mr. Anderson said. "You four will need another day to gather your things before sailing back to the Snows."

"Has it been a week already?" Pete asked. "It seems like we just got here."

"No," George Anderson laughed, "it's been eight days—but up here it's hard to keep track. And here's some good news about Mr. Geetings. The judge said that he's putting him on probation. He'll be able to stay in his cabin on Elliot Bay. Mr. Geetings said that he's already starting a new book—a story about three boys and a girl who meet on an island. Mr. Geetings wants you to come and visit him as often as you can. He says that your adventures should keep him busy for a long, long time.

BOOKS TO READ FOR MORE INFORMATION

Armour, David A. *100 Years at Mackinac*, Mackinac Island, Michigan, 1995.

Armour, David A. *Attack at Michilimackinac*, Mackinac Island, Michigan, 1971.

Clifton, James A., George L. Cornell and James M. McClurken. *People of the Three Fires*, Grand Rapids, Michigan, 1986.

Gringhuis, Dirk. *The Young Voyageur*, Mackinac Island, Michigan, 1955 (reprinted 1996).

McVeigh, Amy. *Mackinac Connection: An Insider's Guide*, Mackinac Island, Michigan, 1992.

Peterson, Eugene T. *Mackinac Island, Its History in Pictures*, Mackinac Island, Michigan, 1972.

Pittman, Philip McM. *The Les Cheneaux Chronicles*, Cedarville, Michigan, 1984.

Porter, Phillip. *Verandas of Mackinac Island*, Mackinac Island, Michigan, 1981.

Williams, Meade C. *Early Mackinac: The Fairy Island*, St. Louis, Missouri, 1897.

Wood, Edwin O. *Historic Mackinac*, New York, New York, 1918.